A Double Life

A YELLOW COTTAGE MYSTERY

J. New

D1519472

OTHER BOOKS BY J. NEW

The Yellow Cottage Vintage Mysteries in order:
The Yellow Cottage Mystery (Free)
An Accidental Murder
The Curse of Arundel Hall
A Clerical Error
The Riviera Affair
A Double Life
The Finch & Fischer Mysteries in order:
Decked in the Hall
Death at the Duck Pond

For my Grandparents.

Chapter One

IT WAS THE SOFT MEWLING sound I heard first. I was approaching the Peter Pan statue in Kensington Park gardens and the October wind had stilled momentarily. I crept forward slowly, trying to ascertain its direction, thinking it must be a small animal in distress. A kitten perhaps that had wandered too far from its mother and found itself lost. But it had stopped.

I waited for a while but apart from the soft susurration of the breeze in the trees all was silent. I was about to leave and return to my brother's new house where I was visiting for a few weeks, thinking I'd imagined it, when the cry came again, louder this time and more of a whimper. It was coming from inside the evergreen bushes that surrounded the statue.

I approached gingerly not wanting to frighten the poor creature, and pushed aside the branches of the Beech, snagging my coat on the Hawthorn and not quite avoiding the sharp thorns which whipped back against my cheek and almost tore the hat from my head.

With my head bent low I pushed further into the foliage, my feet sinking slightly into the sodden ground, when the whimper became a cry.

"Good lord!" I cried out in shock.

I knew exactly what I would find before I hastily pushed aside the final low-hanging branches to reveal a cream wheel with its chromium spokes.

I leaned over the perambulator and peered in at the tightly wrapped bundle inside. Dressed all in blue I assumed it was a little boy. A small face beneath a blue knitted bonnet greeted me, red and scrunched up as he wailed, anxious upon waking and finding himself alone. I laid a hand on his chest through the layers of blankets and spoke in soothing tones. The touch, the sound of my voice, or a combination of the two had the desired effect and the heart-wrenching cries stopped. Blue tearful eyes peered at me beneath long light lashes and the quivering of the chin and lower lip ceased.

"Now then, little one. What on earth are you doing here? Don't worry, you're safe now," I said, gently wiping his wet face with my handkerchief.

As I was talking, I made sure the hood was up properly and fastened in place, then gripped the handle to manoeuvre it out of the shrubbery. It was facing the way I had entered, so a quick shove or two should do it. Releasing the brake on the wheels I once again pushed through the Hawthorn, this time snagging my lisle hose. As I kicked out to free my leg, I felt the tear of the fabric and the sharp scratch which tore the flesh below and fervently wished I had worn my slacks that morning instead of a skirt.

I staggered back onto the empty footpath, and found the wind had once again picked up and was aware of the rumble of thunder in the distance. As I looked up at the thick, leaden clouds a large fat raindrop exploded on my cheek and splashed into my eye.

"Oh dear," I said to the baby who hadn't taken his eyes off me since the moment he'd opened them. "It looks like there's a terrible storm coming. I think it best if I take you back to my house and contact the authorities."

I turned to retrace the route I'd taken earlier, my eyes constantly scanning the area for a panicking nanny or a parent who was looking for a missing child. But with the rain coming down heavily now, the few people who had been taking the air when I'd arrived had disappeared. No doubt heading back to the warmth of hearth and home or the shelter of a nearby coffee shop.

With my sister-in-law Ginny being almost seven months pregnant and resting, and my brother Gerry working on his latest novel, I'd found myself at a loose end more often than not and had taken to daily walks through the large park opposite their new house. But this particular journey, with my added responsibility, seemed to take twice as long as it had at any other time I'd ventured for a stroll around the gardens.

I hurried up Mount Walk, passing the Round Pond on my right and the bandstand on my left, before joining Studio Walk and leaving via Studio Gate. Twenty minutes after I'd pulled the baby free from the bushes, I was back at Brunswick Gardens. I raced up the flight of stone steps and shoved open the door calling for help. Then returned to the baby at the bottom.

The housekeeper arrived almost immediately and gasped at the sight of the pram. Hot on her heels was my brother Gerry.

"What's all the ruckus about?" he asked, peering over the housekeeper's shoulder. "Good Lord, Ella! What have you done now? Is that a baby?"

"Do you think you could help me up with the pram please, Gerry? I'm soaked to the skin. And to answer your questions, I've done nothing, and yes, it is a baby."

AS WE SETTLED THE PRAM in the hall, the grandfather clock struck three-thirty. The door was wrenched from my hand by a sudden gust of wind and slammed shut with a powerful bang, and an almighty boom of thunder cracked overhead, rattling the window panes. Swiftly followed by several flashes of lightning which caused the hall lights to flicker several times, then go off altogether.

The multitude of unfamiliar noises started the baby crying again and Ginny appeared at the top of the stairs asking what all the noise was about. Then her eyes lit on the pram and widened in shock.

"Ella! You've brought a baby home. Whatever for?"

"Well, it was either that or leave him hidden in the bushes in a torrential downpour," I said, unpinning my sodden hat and throwing it on the hall table.

By this time Ginny had made her way carefully down the stairs and was lifting the screaming child into her arms, rocking him gently and cooing. It certainly did the trick and once again he quieted down, peering intensely at this new face with a quizzical frown.

"I say, old girl," said Gerry. "What do you mean by 'leave him in the bushes'?"

"Exactly what I said, Gerry. I found him abandoned in the shrubbery by the Peter Pan statue. No sign of a nanny or parents anywhere within the immediate vicinity, nor en route back here. So I brought him home. Now if you don't mind, I need to get changed. Then I'll call Baxter and see if he's had any reports of a missing child."

Detective Sergeant Baxter was my colleague at Scotland Yard when my consultancy services were required, and we'd worked a number of successful cases together. If anyone could find out to whom the child belonged, it would be him.

"I say, Ella, do you know your face is bleeding and your stocking is ripped?"

"I do, Gerry. I had an argument with a Hawthorn bush."

"Well, at least your shoes match. Ah, no, I spoke too soon."

I glanced down at my feet with a frown. One dark brown shoe (left foot) and one black shoe (right foot) stared back at me. I sighed. It wasn't the first time I'd done this. I'd thought buying the same style of shoe in two different colours was a good idea. Time saving and practical. I wouldn't do it again.

"Well, I can't do anything about it now. Besides, we have more than my fashion sense to worry about."

"Poor little mite. Who would do such a thing?" Ginny said, handing the infant to the housekeeper with instructions to take him to the newly-decorated nursery. "There should be everything you need to make him more comfortable."

"Darling, there's enough in the nursery to make most of the children in the city comfortable," Gerry grinned.

It was true. Ever since they'd been given confirmation of the new addition to the family Ginny had been shopping. I'd had it from Gerry that they now owned a matinee jacket in every colour of the rainbow and had had to purchase a new wardrobe to house it all.

"Oh, Gerry, you do exaggerate," she said with a giggle. "Now, Ella, you go and get changed. You're absolutely drenched, darling. I'll send Betty up to see to your cuts."

"There's no need, I can manage those, but if she could perhaps mend the tear in my coat and see to my shoes? I'm afraid my hose are beyond repair."

"Of course. Ella, do you think I should call Uncle Albert about the baby? The parents must be frantic with worry and he'll know what to do."

Sir Montesford, or Uncle Albert as we knew him, wasn't actually a blood relative but was a good friend of the family as well as being Ginny's Godfather. He was also the Chief of Police and the man responsible for employing me as a consultant detective with Scotland Yard. While I knew beyond a shadow of a doubt that should his favourite Goddaughter telephone asking for his help then he would oblige, but by the same token he was also far too senior an officer to involve in a case such as this. That's what Baxter and I were for. I said as much to Ginny who nodded.

"Yes, I suppose you're right. Besides, I've just remembered he's at the House of Lords today. Tea will be ready in the drawing room when you are."

"Don't worry, Ginny, I'm sure Baxter will reunite the baby with his family lickety-split and that will be the end of it."

"Famous last words," Gerry said with a smile.

I should have listened to him.

———◉———

IN MY ROOM I CLEANED the two small cuts on my face and leg, then hurriedly dried my sodden hair and brushed it into a style not unlike a bird's nest. I glared at it in the looking glass, as though through force of will alone it would miraculously form itself into a sleek and perfectly coiffed style. No such luck. It remained a fright.

I dressed warmly, hoping I hadn't made another fashion faux pas. The lights were still out and with the storm raging outside I could hardly see a thing. I opted to wear my dark pink felt slippers, easily recognised by touch alone, with an interwoven light pink ribbon and bow. Not something I would have chosen for myself but they were a gift from Ginny and remarkably comfortable. It was either those or a second pair of mismatched shoes.

Dashing downstairs, I lifted the telephone receiver in the hall and put a call through to Baxter at The Yard. While I waited Betty, the maid, came up from the kitchen with a laden tea tray and gave me a cheeky smile.

"Cor blimey, Miss Bridges. You've had a day of it, haven't you? A baby! Who'd have thought it. Poor little bairn. I wonder what happened?"

Betty was an excellent maid but chattered like a magpie and like most young under-stair staff loved to gossip. Luckily, I was saved from having to reply when Baxter came on the line. I returned Betty's smile and indicated she should take the tea in before it got cold.

"Hello, Miss Bridges."

"Hello, Baxter, how are you?"

"Fair to middling. How about yourself?"

"Quite well, Baxter, thank you. But I'm afraid this isn't so much a social call."

"Didn't think it would be for a moment, Miss Bridges. How can I help?"

"I've found a baby, Baxter."

There was a slight pause before Baxter cleared his throat.

"A baby? As in...?"

"Yes. A small human being. A boy, I think, as he's dressed all in blue. I found him in his pram in Kensington Park hidden in the bushes by the Peter Pan statue. I wonder if you could see if there's been a report of him missing from his parents or his nanny?"

"Of course. Where is the boy now? He's unharmed I take it?"

"Oh yes, he's fine. I brought him home with me."

"Right. Well, leave it with me, Miss Bridges. I shall make some inquiries and telephone you back if I have something to report."

"Thank you, Baxter."

I gave him the telephone number, then replaced the receiver and joined Gerry and Ginny in the drawing room. The fire was roaring in the grate, giving out much needed warmth and light, and Gerry had lit candles while we waited for the electricity to come back on.

Ginny poured me a cup of tea and rested it on a side table while I helped myself to the array of sandwiches and cakes. As to be expected the conversation centered around the extraordinary goings-on of that afternoon.

"I'm shocked that someone would do that to a small baby," Ginny said, nibbling on a French fancy. "Or any child for that matter."

"We don't know what happened yet. Perhaps they thought they were keeping him safe?" I said.

"But from what? What possible danger could there be in the palace gardens?"

"I really don't know, Ginny. I'm as baffled as you are."

"It's all dashed odd," Gerry said, lashing his scone with strawberry preserve. I'd brought it with me. The fruit had been picked from my own garden on Linhay Island and my former housekeeper, Mrs Parsons, had made the jam. "I mean what would have happened if you'd not found him? A torrential rain pour like this with the Long Water just behind where he was found. My God, he could have..."

"Oh, Gerry don't!" cried Ginny. Then to my surprise promptly burst into tears.

This was a side to Ginny I had never seen. She was unfailingly a positive person who always looked on the bright side and saw humour in almost everything. In fact, more often than not she took things far less seriously than she ought on occasion. And while Gerry had warned me it may happen, according to their Doctor it was perfectly normal for a woman in her condition to be prone to bouts of hysteria, it still came as a shock to me.

Gerry jumped up and sat by her side, holding her close and apologising for his tactless remark. Ginny rallied quickly and sniffed, delicately patting her eyes with her handkerchief.

"Oh dear. I'm so sorry. I can't seem to help it."

I told her not to fret so, her response was perfectly normal.

"I found him in ample time, darling. Call it fate or serendipity, but the fact is he's safe and I'm sure Baxter will telephone soon to say he's found the child's parents. Then he can go home."

Just then, as though he'd heard me across London, the telephone bell rang and Betty came to tell me Baxter was on the line.

"Hello again, Miss Bridges. Baxter here with some news. Apparently at three-thirty a Mr James Parfitt stopped a police constable in the Italian Gardens a bit further north from where you found the baby. Almost pulled him off his bicycle by all accounts. Anyway, he was most agitated, saying his baby son and the nanny were missing."

I brought the map of Kensington Palace gardens to mind. Yes, I travelled west to return home so mine and the father's paths wouldn't have crossed.

"Does he live close by?" I asked.

"Yes, in Mayfair. The constable accompanied him home and I've been in touch personally to inform him the boy has been found. I'll come and collect him myself and take him home."

"Alright. Thank you, Baxter. Do you know how it happened by the way? I mean it's not every day a baby is abandoned in the park."

"Not as yet. I'll know more when I see Mr Parfitt. Unfortunately, the nanny is still unaccounted for."

⸻ ◉ ⸻

THREE-QUARTERS OF AN hour later Baxter arrived at the door. And divested of his coat, hat and umbrella was shown into the drawing room by Betty where I waited for him. Gerry had gone back to his writing and Ginny was upstairs with the baby.

"Hello, Baxter. Come in and get warm by the fire. Apologies for the gloom, I'm afraid the lights have gone out. Something to do with the storm I expect. Would you like some tea?"

Baxter shook his head. "I partook of a cuppa at The Yard before I came out. But I'll take you up on the seat by the fire, it's raging a good one out there. Tree limbs are down all over and half of London has lost power. It's a good job you found the bairn when you did, Miss Bridges. That's all I can say."

Once settled he took out his notebook and pencil.

"So, can you tell me what happened?"

It took me less than ten minutes to recount my movements up to finding the baby, and the hurried return journey while I tried to outrun the pending storm.

"'The clock struck the half hour as I got through the door. I just made it before the heavens opened thoroughly.'"

"And you saw no one fitting a nanny's description in the vicinity of the statue?"

"I saw no one at all, Baxter, nanny or otherwise. The wind had got up and the rain had started. Not to mention the deafening rumbles of thunder. It was apparent a heavy storm was imminent and people had left to find shelter. You've not found her then?"

Baxter finished recording my statement and returned his notebook to his inside jacket pocket.

"I'm afraid not. Her name's Josephine Brown and according to Mrs Elizabeth Parfitt she wouldn't have disappeared intentionally, especially while being in charge of the boy. She adores Rupert, that's the bairn's name by the way, and is a most responsible and trustworthy member of staff. She can't think what's happened but is adamant it must be something dreadful."

"Are your men still searching?" I asked, thinking how impossible it must be with the weather as it was.

"No. I've had to call it off. I've risked them enough as it is. We'll start again as soon as it's light. Assuming the storm has blown itself out by then."

He rose from his chair eager to be on his way and I rang the bell for Betty. She appeared so quickly it was obvious she'd been hovering in the hall. I frowned at her, letting her know I was aware of her eavesdropping. She looked suitably abashed, but I knew her contriteness wouldn't last.

"Betty, please tell Mrs Bridges that Detective Baxter will return the baby now."

The maid ran up the stairs and I helped Baxter on with his coat.

"Are you walking across the park in this, Baxter? We do have the child's pram but even so it will be a terrible ordeal."

"Don't you fret, Miss Bridges. I have a car and a driver waiting at the kerb. I'll take the boy back on his own and make arrangements for the pram to be collected and returned to the parents later."

As Ginny handed over the baby and thanked Baxter, I conveyed my hopes that he would find the nanny in good health soon and put an end to the mystery.

"I hope so too, Miss Bridges," he said. "I really do."

Chapter Two

GERRY, GINNY AND I all took breakfast together in the orangerie the next morning. Then, as had been the routine for the
week so far, Gerry retired to the library to work on his latest
novel and Ginny to her upstairs salon. She was currently organ-
ising the New Year's Eve ball at the Dorchester.

I had just poured myself a second cup of coffee when Betty
entered.

"Detective Baxter to see you, miss."

"Good morning, Baxter," I said, as he strode into the room.
"I didn't expect to see you again so soon. Have you come for the
pram?"

"The pram? Oh, no it's another matter."

The look on his face told me it wasn't happy news. "Sit
down and have a cup of coffee and tell me what's happened. I
can tell the news isn't good. Is it the nanny? Have you found
her?"

"We've found a body, Miss Bridges. Female. Too early to say
whether it's definitely Josephine Brown, but it's probable under
the circumstances."

"Oh, Baxter, no," I said in dismay. "When was she found?"

Baxter glanced at his wristwatch. "About a quarter of an
hour ago. I hurried here as soon as the alarm was sounded.
We're waiting on the pathologist now."

"Where was she found?"

"Trapped under the Serpentine Bridge."

The bridge marked the boundary between Hyde Park and Kensington Gardens. The Serpentine Lake was recreational and created at the behest of Queen Caroline in 1730. The Long water was the name given to the long and narrow western half of the lake. And it was directly behind where I'd found the child.

"Initial thoughts are she slipped, banged her head and fell unconscious into the Long Water," Baxter continued. "Then the current, which I admit has been faster than normal due to the rain and the storm, swept her down to the bridge."

"But you don't think that's what happened?"

He shook his head. "No, I don't."

"And nor do I. It can't have been an accident because if that were the case the pram would have been left in the open. Yet it was hidden quite cleverly and to my mind deliberately. Once again, Baxter, it looks as though you and I have a murder to solve."

***

IF I HAD WONDERED AT all about the strength of the previous night's storm, walking through Kensington Gardens that morning left me with no doubt whatsoever.

The scenes of devastation and destruction were everywhere. The wind had whipped up to an unprecedented level overnight, which had kept me awake until the early hours. Now the remnants of windows, roof tiles and broken bricks lay in the street.

We skirted the obstructions, including a small newspaper kiosk which had been blown over and had come to a stop against the park railing. Yards from where it normally stood.

Sodden newspapers and magazines littered the street and were caught high up in tree branches.

As we neared the gate to the park, we saw several well-established trees had been uprooted and lay across the pathways and lawns. Incongruously the sky was a pale blue and a weak sun was beginning to shine.

The constable guarding the gate nodded deferentially to my colleague and let us through. There was a constable on each gate, Baxter informed me, and the gardens were closed.

The heavy rain had left behind large puddles and a handful of areas were flooded and impassable. Already there were several crews made up of men from the London Fire Brigade, police and locals hard at work beginning the clear up, the Kensington Palace gardeners directing efforts. I had no doubt that if the devastation I could see around me extended to the rest of London and beyond, the army would be drafted in to help directly. Although the area around the bridge had been declared a crime scene with no access to anyone but the police. Luckily our route was relatively straightforward.

"Good heavens, Baxter, I've never seen such damage from a storm in my life. I do hope my cottage is alright."

My home was on Linhay Island at the very Southern end of the country, and barely a stone's throw from the English Channel.

"Well, I believe the South West caught the brunt of it before it moved inland so you may have escaped the worst. Let's hope so, eh?"

"Yes, indeed. Thank you, Baxter."

There really was nothing I could do. Although I would telephone my housekeeper later to check she and my other staff were unscathed.

As we neared the Serpentine Bridge, I could see several police constables milling about on the bank. The body had come to rest close to the shore line thankfully, trapped by a boulder at the base of the nearest of the five arches.

"Has the pathologist arrived yet?" Baxter called down.

"Not yet, sir."

While Baxter scrambled down the slippery bank to speak with his men, I happened to glance up at the bridge to see a forlorn figure staring back at me, wearing a familiar uniform. It was the ghost of the nanny whose body lay trapped in the water below.

My purchase of the Yellow Cottage on Linhay, a place I had first fallen in love with as a child, had come with a rather unusual gift: the ability to see spirits. In particular those whose lives had ended in suspicious circumstances. They appeared to me, and me only, in their quest for help in solving the mysteries of their untimely deaths. It had changed the direction of my life completely and was the very reason I had become a consultant detective with Scotland Yard in the first place.

So far the cases I had been involved in I had managed to solve successfully. With no small help from Baxter and my Aunt Margaret. I only hoped I could do the same for Josephine Brown.

<hr>

A FEW MINUTES AFTER descending the slope to the level bank, Baxter turned and raised a hand. I was just about to answer his wave when I realised I wasn't the intended recipient. I looked behind me to see Doctor Mortimer Smythe, the police surgeon, loping towards us. His long legs eating up the ground twice as fast as mine had done.

"Well, well, well, Miss Bridges. This is a surprise. How are you?"

"I believe the correct response is fair to middling, Doctor Smythe," I said as Baxter joined us. "How have you been?"

He laughed. "You've been working with Baxter for too long. I'm well, thank you for asking. Which is more than I can say for this poor soul," he said, nodding at the body in the water.

As he spoke, I saw movement to his rear and leaned back to see a black four-legged shape with green eyes staring at me. It was my cat Phantom. Another of the gifts that had come with my cottage, and also a spirit. Mortimer, noticing my gaze, looked in the same direction but of course saw nothing.

"Something of interest, Ella?"

"No. I was just gauging the distance from where I found the baby."

Mortimer started. "Baby? You don't mean I have two bodies to deal with?"

"Oh, I'm terribly sorry, Mortimer. No, the baby is fine. I found him abandoned yesterday and took him home. Baxter has already reunited him with his parents."

"We think the body down there is the nanny," Baxter explained.

"Ah, I see. Right, well let me get down there and we'll see what's what, shall we?"

While I had managed to put on matching shoes that morning they were thoroughly impractical for this sort of business. However, the alternative was a pair of wellington boots which belonged to Gerry, Ginny not owning any, and stuffed with several pairs of socks to make them fit better. Not a viable option as far as I was concerned. So, with the aid of Baxter I managed to slip and slide myself down the bank without falling, much to my relief.

Baxter and I stood out of the way while Mortimer directed the constables in the safe and gentle removal of the body from the water onto higher ground. Then, they too stood a respectful distance away and let the pathologist do his work.

We had only been observing for a few minutes when there was a shout from further up the bank. A constable who had been scouring along the edge of the Long Water was waving his arms.

"Looks like one of my lads has found something," Baxter said. "We'll leave you to it, Mortimer. Back shortly."

———◦———

THE LONG WATER STARTED at The Italian Gardens to the North of the park and stretched down to the bridge. Beyond, it joined the Serpentine lake.

Not quite half way between the two, nearer to the North side, was the statue of J. M. Barrie's Peter Pan, deliberately concealed within the foliage. It was where I had discovered the baby. It was also where the constable now stood awaiting our arrival.

We walked in single file, Baxter taking the lead and me bringing up the rear. Between us Phantom stalked along, head and tail both held high with what I could only surmise was disdain. He practically vibrated with annoyance and I was sure he rolled his eyes at me at least once.

"How was I supposed to know you were trying to attract my attention?" I hissed quietly. But not quietly enough.

"Did you say something, Miss Bridges?" Baxter called from a yard or two in front.

"Nothing important. Just thinking out loud."

Phantom stalked on, ignoring me, then as we reached the waiting policeman, disappeared into thin air. His job was done.

"What have you got for me then, Pike?" Baxter asked.

"A handbag, sir," he replied from the bank below. "It's caught on a branch down there. I haven't touched it."

"Good man."

"Is it in the water, constable?" I asked.

"Partly, miss."

"We need to retrieve it, Baxter, before the contents are completely ruined."

I felt around in my pocket for a handkerchief and held it out for the waiting officer. He climbed a couple of feet up the bank and took it from my outstretched hand.

"Thread it through the handle and then try to loosen it. If there are fingerprints to be found we don't want to obliterate them with our own."

"Yes, miss."

"And try not to fall in, Pike. I don't relish the idea of coming in to rescue you."

Pike grimaced. "No fear, sir. I can't swim."

He carefully inched his way back to the water's edge while Baxter and I took a cursory glance around the vicinity. Baxter picked up a fallen branch and thrust aside the foliage on either side of the footpath until he came to something of note.

"Looks like there could have been a bit of a scuffle here," he said, pointing to the bushes a little further beyond those I'd been in yesterday. I had a look and had to agree with him.

"Yes, it's possible. Especially considering it's right where the baby was hidden. But with the storm last night it could just as easily have been damage from that. We'll need to have a closer look, Baxter. See if anything in the way of evidence can be found. Footprints are obviously out due to the layer of leaves and the soaked ground, but something might have been dropped."

Baxter nodded. "I'll get Pike and another man to go through it. They can have a look at where the pram was hidden too."

"Got it, sir," Pike said from behind us and handed the handkerchief to Baxter, the bag swinging below, water draining out onto the footpath.

"Well done, Pike."

"I say. That's a jolly expensive handbag for a nanny," I said, looking at it more closely. "If I'm not mistaken, it's a Cartier!"

In between the case of a murdered vicar at the church fete and rushing off to the Riviera to help my mother with a missing friend, I'd been involved in helping a fashion house whose designs were being copied. It had helped tremendously with my knowledge of fashion. Even though I was predisposed to taking comfort and practicality over what was deemed popular myself.

"I see," said Baxter. Who I could tell by his voice didn't, really.

"It's worth hundreds of pounds, Baxter."

"For a handbag?"

"It's a luxury item. And certainly not one your average nanny could afford."

"Well, that's certainly curious. But we'll know as soon as we open it whether it's hers or not. I'll give it to Mortimer, he's got all the gubbins necessary to do it properly. Now, Pike, I have another job for you and Robins. I'll send him over shortly."

While Baxter explained to the eager constable the possibility of a second crime scene, and the various instructions he was to adhere to, I began to wander back in the direction of the bridge. I was hoping Mortimer would have the information we needed by this time.

Chapter Three

BAXTER CAUGHT UP WITH me just as I reached the scene of the crime and together we approached Mortimer, who was just packing his bag while the body of Josephine Brown was being loaded onto a stretcher. She was covered with a blanket and would be carried to the ambulance waiting just outside the park gates.

Mortimer snapped his Gladstone shut and joined us on the upper bank. Tapping various pockets, he eventually brought forth his pipe, a ritual I was now familiar with, and after filling it with Old Holborn and tamping it down, he then spent a few minutes getting it alight. Several puffs later, when he knew it was safe to speak, Baxter asked the question.

"What's the verdict then, Mortimer?"

"I'll know more when I get to the morgue of course, but preliminary findings are she was strangled with something. A length of wire or cord of some sort, then her body was thrown into the water. Somewhere up there," he said, indicating where we'd just come from. "No sign that she put up much of a struggle. Could be she was taken by surprise from behind, or knew her attacker and he struck once she'd turned her back on him. But she's been in the water a while so any surface evidence to that effect will have been washed away most likely. She was also wearing gloves which will have protected her hands somewhat. I'll have a better look later."

"Any identification on her?" I asked.

"None. Pockets are empty and there's no sign of a handbag. Ah..." he said when Baxter raised his hand. "I'll take that with me and let you have it back later with my full report."

"Can you estimate a time of death?" Baxter said, laying the handbag on the passing stretcher.

"I can give you quite a good one as a matter of fact. Her wristwatch had stopped at two-thirty, probably the moment it was submerged in the water."

"Two-thirty?" I stammered.

It should have occurred to me before, but with the shock of finding the baby and the urgency to get him to safety before the storm started, it had never even crossed my mind.

"That poor woman was lying in the water directly behind me yesterday!"

"Now, now, Miss Bridges," Mortimer said gently, taking my elbow and guiding me away from the bridge. He spoke as we walked, "There was nothing you could have done. She was already dead by the time you found the child. And even if you had known, what could you have done except take the child to safety and call Baxter? Exactly what you did do. If you'd waited any longer, you would have been putting both yourself and the baby at high risk with a storm of that magnitude imminent. You did the only sensible and correct thing, my dear, there's no need to chastise yourself."

He was right of course. I'd taken the only course of action available to me at the time. My priority had been the safety of Rupert Parfitt.

"Thank you, Mortimer."

"You're welcome, my dear. Now, I believe this is where we part ways," he said as we reached Mount Gate. "I'll have my report to you this afternoon, Baxter. Cheerio."

Mortimer would exit at Alexander Gate where the ambulance was parked on Kensington Road and Baxter and I would follow Mount Walk and leave the way we had entered, via Studio Gate. He stopped momentarily to speak to his men. Telling them to be on the look-out for a piece of wire or cord which could have been used as the murder weapon. He called over a young constable, Robins, telling him to pass the message onto Pike and to help him scour the area where the victim was most likely killed.

Neither Baxter nor myself held out much hope that the murder weapon would be found though, especially if it had been thrown in the water. But a search needed to be done as part of a thorough investigation.

He walked me back to the house, and we made arrangements to meet at his Scotland Yard office that afternoon, to go through the pathologist's report and the contents of the handbag. Hopefully they would provide us with a clue as to how to proceed.

<hr>

AFTER LUNCH AND A MUCH needed cup of tea, I telephoned home to see how things were.

While I had been in the Riviera my temporary housekeeper Mrs Parsons had found me a perfect replacement. Miss Bertha Popkin, known to all at her own request as simply Popkin, was the elder sister of our greengrocer Walter and rented a small home not far from the main street.

A spinster, she'd been looking after the needs of her brother for many years but Walter had recently got married so she had been seeking new employment. With staff accommodation available at my cottage and very happy in her new role, she was seriously considering giving notice to the rental agent and moving in.

After the third ring she answered.

"Hello, Popkin, it's Ella. I'm just calling to see if everything is alright after the storm?"

"Hello, Miss Bridges. Don't worry, everything's in hand. Just a few slates off the roof and a couple of panes broken in the greenhouses, but Tom's fixing those. It will all be as good as new by the time you get back."

"And nobody was hurt?"

"Oh no, we were all sensible enough to stay indoors until it was over. We're all as right as bobbins, Miss Bridges."

"I'm very pleased to hear it. And how did the rest of Linhay fair?"

"In the main not too bad, but sadly one of the old wooden classrooms at the Suntrap School blew down completely."

The Suntrap School was a special residential school dedicated to helping frail and sick children from the inner city areas. Most suffered from asthma, rheumatic heart, minor degrees of emotional disturbance and varying degrees of physical disability. It belonged to the Borough of Tottenham and offered a wide variety of education facilities as well as being situated in very pleasant surroundings, which were extremely conducive to the improvement of the children's health and well-being. My gardener Tom put forth an idea to me early on in his employment, to donate the surplus fruit and vegetables from our Victorian walled garden to the school. An idea I was very happy to agree to.

"Oh, that's not good news, Popkin. I hope no one was hurt?"

"Unfortunately, the cookery teacher, Mrs Blenkinsop, went out the next day and had a nasty tumble on the debris. Broken her leg, I'm afraid."

"Oh dear, the poor woman. Is she recovering well?"

"The doctor came right away and fixed her up temporarily until they could get her to hospital. She's there now and is in cheerful spirits, but she's decided to finally retire. She said she should have done it years ago, but she loves the children dearly. Anyway, when she's allowed to leave hospital, she's off to live with her sister in Wales."

"They'll be looking for someone to replace her then?"

"Oh yes, but not until they get things cleared up and a new classroom built so the headmaster tells me."

"Well, if they need a volunteer, I'm sure Tom will be more than happy to help."

"I'll let him know."

We chattered on for a few minutes more, Popkin telling me of how the community was all banding together to help one another, then said our goodbyes. I spent a peaceful hour or so reading and catching up on correspondence before it was time to leave for my meeting with Baxter.

———— ◦ ————

BY QUARTER PAST THREE that afternoon, Baxter and I were ensconced in his office at Scotland Yard, perusing Mortimer's preliminary report. I had brought pastries and my colleague had provided tea in a Brown Betty pot along with two cups. The one without the chip in the rim he handed to me.

"Everything alright at home, Miss Bridges?"

"Yes, thankfully. According to my housekeeper a few roof tiles are missing and several of the greenhouse panes have been broken. But apart from those, which my gardener is in the process of fixing, all seems to be well. The island has come together to help one another, though the full brunt of the storm missed Linhay thankfully. I'll know more when I return home of course. But I suspect it will all be done and dusted by that point."

"Well, let's hope this case can be solved in as timely a manner."

The power still hadn't come on so we were working by the light of two stubby candles and an oil lantern which were placed on the desk.

Sipping our tea and munching on pastries we read the report together in silence. It made for rather gruesome reading and I pushed away the last morsel of pastry as my appetite evaporated.

"So, according to Mortimer she did put up an initial fight if the marks across her fingers are anything to go by," Baxter said.

"Yes. Poor woman. I wonder what she could have possibly done to warrant such an act?"

"We'll need to know more about her to answer that question. I've told James and Elizabeth Parfitt we'll be along later."

I nodded. "As for the monster who's responsible, I have no words strong enough to describe him. Not only did he murder this poor nanny, but he left a baby stranded and hidden in appalling weather. What sort of callous individual would do such a thing, Baxter? It's reprehensible."

"It is, Miss Bridges. But rest assured we'll catch him. I for one shan't rest until he's behind bars. Now, while I remember, I needed a formal identification. With no personal effects to be found on her person and a handbag that may not have been hers, I telephoned Mr Parfitt. In the first instance to inform him we'd found a body which we believed to be his nanny and to pass on our condolences. However, I asked if he'd be willing to come in and confirm it was her."

"And did he do so?"

"Yes. He left half an hour before you arrived. It is indeed Miss Josephine Brown. He also confirmed the handbag as being hers. It had formerly belonged to his wife apparently, which is how he recognised it. She gifted it to Miss Brown on the purchase of a new one for herself."

"I see. Well, that's the lesser mystery solved. Have you had a look at the contents yet?"

"No, I was waiting for you. We may as well do that now. I don't think Mortimer's report can tell us anything more at this stage."

While Baxter tidied away the report, I retrieved the handbag from the spare chair. Mortimer had carefully extracted the contents and dried each piece before sending it all back to us. This made our job a lot easier. Remarkably there was very little damage to anything.

The first item was a bookmark from Hatchards, the oldest book shop in London and one I knew well.

"I'll follow that up, Baxter. I'm a frequent visitor when I'm in the city and know the owner well. Gerry always has his book signings there when he has a new release."

I put it in my bag and made a note in my notebook.

The second item was a plain white handkerchief from which we gleaned nothing, so it was set aside. Followed by a small coin purse containing a few coins, a pressed flower, a pansy by the look of it, a brown button and a driving license in its familiar dark red cover.

Baxter flipped it open.

"Unusual for her to be able to drive, do you think?" I asked.

"Possibly her employer arranged it. She was obviously well thought of. It's her's alright. Miss Josephine Brown, aged thirty-seven. Valid for another five months. I'll set someone to search for her next-of-kin. I think London's the best place to start then move outward from there if we find nothing."

"It will be difficult with nothing more to go on," I said. "Brown is a common name."

"You never know we might have some luck. Hopefully the Parfitts can shed more light on the matter. Is that it for the bag?"

I rummaged around inside the various compartments. "Yes, I think so. Oh, wait. The lining is torn a little at the bottom of the central portion. Could you hold the light over here a moment?"

I held the bag up at an angle while Baxter kindly held the lamp in position.

"It's not torn at all. It's been carefully cut. And there's something inside. Whatever it is has been deliberately concealed. This could be the clue we need, Baxter!"

———— ◆ ————

"HOW UNUSUAL THAT MORTIMER missed this," I said, retrieving my tweezers from my own handbag.

"Well, apart from it being easy to miss, he was doing us a favour. Bodies are his job, not handbags. I suspect he asked one of his staff to do it."

"Yes, you could very well be right."

I inserted the tweezers into the small hole in the lining and pulled out a piece of thick, slightly damp paper the shape and length of a cigarette. Putting it on Baxter's desk blotter, I carefully unrolled it and we read what was written inside.

"Well, that was worth waiting for," Baxter said.

I stared at him and he returned the look, his eyes filled with mirth. I laughed. "Oh, very good, Baxter." It was so unlike him to use sarcasm and his timing was impeccable. But he did have a point, it appeared to be complete nonsense.

'A manille twofolds a tinnily foursquare.

Threesome, seniles, puniness'

"What on earth does it mean, Baxter?"

He took his time to reply, obviously thinking hard.

"As a whole I have no idea. The individual words themselves?... I have no idea either."

I sighed. "Nor I. Do you have a dictionary to hand?"

He opened the bottom drawer of his desk and handed me a small cloth-bound book.

"It must be some sort of code. Perhaps the meaning of each individual word will help?"

I turned to the M's. "Oh, Manille is a card game played with thirty-two cards and originating in France. Take notes, Baxter, if you would."

"Yes, Miss."

"Sorry, Baxter."

I turned to the T's. "Twofold is something which has two parts or does two things at once. And Tinnily relates to or resembles tin. While threesome is a game or activity for three people."

I didn't think we were getting anywhere at all, but pushed on and found seniles to mean showing a loss of cognitive abilities. Puniness, a quality of being unimportant, frivolous or petty, although I personally felt those could hardly be described as qualities. Foursquare was an adjective which meant something consisting of four corners or four right angles.

I glanced across at Baxter's notebook.

"So, we're possibly looking for one or three unimportant, frivolous and petty Frenchmen, who've lost their marbles and like to play two games of cards around a square table while eating tinned food?"

"Or, we could be grasping at straws."

"Yes, that too. But it must mean something or why go to such lengths to conceal it?"

"We'll have to work on it another time, I'm afraid, Miss Bridges. We're due to speak to the Parfitts. I have a driver waiting. And for what it's worth, I suggest we don't mention what we've found for the time being. Agreed?"

"Absolutely. No mention of secret notes, tinned goods or Frenchmen."

⸺⬤⸺

BAXTER HADN'T GIVEN the Parfitts a definitive time for the interview, so, to all intents and purposes we arrived unannounced. The door was opened by a butler who led us into the drawing room and asked us to wait while he fetched the lady of the house. She arrived a couple of minutes later.

"Apologies for leaving you waiting, Detective Baxter, I've just been settling Rupert. In light of what happened I find myself loath to leave him. And you must be Miss Bridges?"

She came and took my hands in hers and looked at me with moist eyes.

"How can I ever thank you enough for finding my son? I'm so very grateful that God saw fit to put you in the right place at the very time you would be required. If there is anything at all you ever need, please do ask. I-we-are permanently in your debt."

I smiled and gently squeezed her hands, "There's no need to be, Mrs Parfitt. I'm just glad I was there."

She nodded, then released my hands and indicated we should sit. "Can I get you some tea?"

We both declined the offer.

"Is your husband home, Mrs Parfitt?" Baxter asked.

"He'll be on his way. I asked Higgins to telephone The Foreign Office and leave a message that you'd arrived. He shouldn't be too long."

"Is it alright if we proceed without him?"

"Of course. Please, ask your questions."

"Well, firstly we're having difficulty locating a next-of-kin for Miss Brown. Do you happen to know anything about her family?"

"I'm sorry, no I don't. I was rather under the impression that she didn't have any close relatives left. Parents deceased, and no siblings was my understanding. She never really spoke about anything of a personal nature, you see. In hindsight I think I rather assumed that was the case."

"And how long was she in your employ?" I asked.

"Almost a year and a half. She came to us from an agency two weeks before Rupert was born and fitted in straight away. She was an absolute Godsend. I don't know how I'll ever replace her."

"Did you arrange for her to learn to drive?"

"Yes. Although it turned out to be more of a formality as she was a natural according to her instructor. It didn't take her long to obtain her licence. I don't drive, you see, and with James working so much I felt it prudent to have someone on hand who could in case of an emergency. She used to take Rupert and I to the country for picnics when the weather was good. And she's driven us to my parents in Hereford twice for short stays." She dabbed her eyes with a lace handkerchief. "Oh dear, I miss her terribly."

I glanced at Baxter who caught my eye and cleared his throat.

"Are you sure you're alright to continue, Mrs Parfitt? We'd be quite happy to wait until your husband returns."

"No, I'm fine, honestly. I think it's just suddenly occurred to me I'll not see her again. Please, do go on."

"You gifted her a handbag?" I said.

"That's right. A Cartier."

"Can I ask if you're sure it was empty before you did so?"

"Absolutely. I went through it myself."

I made a note. At least we now had confirmation the hidden note wasn't there before Josephine Brown took possession of the bag.

"What can you tell us about Miss Brown's routine? Did she walk through the park regularly?" Baxter said.

"Every day except Sunday, which was her own day. She left at two o'clock and returned promptly at four for tea."

I frowned as something swirled in the recesses of my mind. But before I could grasp what it was the man of the house returned. He was as dark as his wife was fair.

"So, what have I missed?" he asked the room at large. It was his wife who answered.

"Nothing much, darling. The police have just been asking about nanny driving for me and the handbag I gave her."

James Parfitt nodded and took a seat beside his wife.

"So, what else do you need to know?" he asked.

"Did Miss Brown come with references? And if so did you follow them up?"

"That's my wife's duty," he informed us. Then turned to Elizabeth. "Darling?"

"Oh, yes. An excellent reference from her previous employer. I telephoned and spoke to her myself. I'll get the details for you."

She lifted the roll-top of a small writing bureau set in the alcove next to the fireplace and brought out a small telephone book. Turning to the correct page, she handed it to Baxter who copied the details, then returned it to her.

"Thank you," he said. "Now, if you could show us to Miss Brown's room, please."

———●———

"WHY DO YOU NEED TO go there?" James Parfitt asked. His tone was a little more belligerent than I liked. Why wouldn't he be willing to let us view her room? We were trying to solve her murder and it could contain an important clue. Not to mention we needed to find her family. "We can pack up her belongings and send them on to wherever you say, if that's the reason?"

I stood up and fixed him with a piercing glare. "No, Mr Parfitt, that's not the reason. It's paramount we find out who her people are so we can inform them of her passing. There may be something in her room which will help us locate them. Now, if you'd be so kind as to lead the way."

I could tell James Parfitt was rather taken aback at the severity of my tone, but he'd needed the jolt.

He stood up and ran a hand through his thick dark hair. "I really am terribly sorry. It came out a little sharper than I meant it to. It's all been rather a shock. What with nearly losing my son, the death of Brown under, well let's face it, bally awful circumstances. Then having to identify her earlier... well, I hadn't realised how much it had affected me until now."

I softened a little at his words and his sickly countenance. Knowing a person in real life then having to identify the same on a morgue table is a dreadful thing for anyone to have to do. But I was still confused at his initial attitude and a bit suspicious.

"Of course, Mr Parfitt. I understand."

"God! I've just realised it must have been you who found Rupert and I never even thanked you."

"There's no need, your wife did so on behalf of both of you."

"Well, if there's anything you need, anything at all, please do ask. We owe you a great debt. Now, if you'll follow me, the nanny's rooms are on the next floor."

The Parfitts led while Baxter and I brought up the rear. Baxter winked at me, letting me know silently he had approved of the way I had handled James Parfitt.

As to be expected, Josephine Brown's rooms were situated next to the nursery and linked by a connecting door. While Baxter and I entered the small sitting room to begin our search, Mrs Parfitt went to check on her son. Mr Parfitt remained at the open door, watching us proceed. It wasn't necessary and I found his presence disconcerting. Perhaps he thought we'd steal something if we were not under his watchful eye? Baxter was ignoring him which was obviously the best approach. I decided to move next door.

I left Baxter searching the drawers of a writing desk while I ventured into the bedroom. It consisted of a single bed with a side table and lamp. A wardrobe and a single wing-back armchair propped against the wall. There was nothing in the way of personal knick-knacks which could tell us a little more about the woman to whom the room had belonged. The only decorative touch was a small painting of a child kneeling by a bed in prayer. I suspected it belonged to the Parfitts.

I started on the wardrobe. Inside was a change of uniform and two dresses. One for Winter and the other for warmer weather. Neither of which were fashionable or decorative. Two pairs of sensible shoes were on a rack at the bottom. One black and one brown. Two plain hats, the empty boxes for which were stacked next to the shoes, and a pair of gloves. A medium-weight dark grey coat and a hand-knitted scarf in bottle green completed the contents. I systematically went through the pockets of each item. Checked inside the shoes and the accessories but found nothing.

Similarly, there was nothing to be found in the bedside table drawer, nor underneath the mattress or the bed. The two small brown suitcases on top of the wardrobe were also empty.

I moved back to the sitting room where Baxter had also finished his search and come up empty handed too. James Parfitt was still at the door observing us intently but saying nothing.

The fireplace was set but not lit. A small wireless sat on a book shelf on top of the single book; a cursory glance showed it to be The *Thirty-nine Steps*. Not one I had read. I wondered what on earth she did in her evenings.

I turned to the Parfitts, Elizabeth having joined her husband at the door, and asked about Miss Brown's hobbies, her friends and what she did on her days off We needed a better picture of the life the woman had led if we were to find out why she was killed. I noticed the hard, arrogant look on James Parfitt's face had softened considerably at the return of his wife. Interesting.

"She had Sundays off and one evening a week," Mrs Parfitt said. "Usually Wednesdays, though on occasion she did ask to change it. She either went to the picture house or the theatre as far as I know. I assumed the reason for changing her evening was so she could take in a particular picture or play that she would have missed otherwise. I didn't enquire any further. What she did in her own time was really none of my business."

"What about friends?" Baxter said. "Any visitors here at all?"

"No, she never had visitors come to the house. As to friends, well, I'm afraid I have no idea. As I mentioned earlier, she was an excellent worker but terribly private, and I respected that about her."

"Odd though, now you mention it," James Parfitt said. "I mean, what sort of person doesn't have friends?"

"Oh, James, I'm sure she had friends. Just not ones who came to the house."

For a second the look on James Parfitt's face was one of intense irritation at his wife's comment. Then it disappeared as quickly as it had arrived. He turned to us with a smile.-

"Is that all for now?"

With nothing more to be learned Baxter and I thanked the Parfitts and left. The police driver dropped me off at my door and Baxter and I said goodnight.

I retired that evening knowing I didn't like James Parfitt very much, there was something *off* about him, but also with the nagging thought that I had missed something of significance. I was right, but it wouldn't come to me until much later.

Chapter Four

THE THREE OF US BREAKFASTED in the orangerie the next morning. The clean up outside resulting from the storm was still ongoing, but much of the debris had been cleared away from our immediate area. We had apparently lost several of the roofing slates, however, and a handyman was coming shortly to replace them. The power had also come back on at some point during the night which was good news.

"I say," said Gerry. "Where's the strawberry preserve this morning?"

"You've polished it off, Gerry. Ella and I barely had a look in. You'll have to make do with marmalade this morning."

"Golly, have I really? Well, suffice to say it was scrumptious, Ella. Bring more next time, will you?"

"If you're very good, I'll pop into Fortnum and Mason and get you some. I'm visiting Hatchards next door this morning."

"Are you really? Give George my regards, will you?"

"Is it something to do with the case you're working on, Ella?" Ginny asked.

I explained about the bookmark we'd found in the nanny's handbag.

"We're rather short on clues at present, I'm afraid. This was really the only tangible thing we had to work with. So, I told Baxter I'd go and see George Palmer as I know him personally. We really are in the dark at the moment so I'm hoping he can help."

"Well, give it time, old girl," Gerry said. "I have every faith in you. You've not failed yet."

"Thank you for the vote of confidence. I hope you're right."

With very little more I could tell them, I asked Ginny how the plans for the New Year's Eve ball were coming along. It had been almost a year in the planning, Ginny having agreed to do it before becoming pregnant. Now, of course, it was unlikely she'd be able to attend herself, but with her truly giving spirit, her love of a good party and an address book which read like an edition of Who's Who, she'd thrown herself wholeheartedly into its organisation. If the guest list was anything to go by, it would most likely be the party of the year, if not the decade.

Ginny herself of course had been Lady Virginia prior to marrying my brother. Now, although she was Lady Virginia Bridges, she much preferred plain old Mrs Bridges. It was a sobriquet she adored, although her mother still insisted on the correct protocol and introduced her in public as a Lady whenever the opportunity arose. Ginny counted various Lords and Ladies as personal friends, not to mention minor royalty, both domestic and foreign, all of whom would be attending The Dorchester at the end of the year. I was looking forward to it immensely. Not least because Jacques, a man I had become close to in France, had confirmed his attendance and I hadn't seen him since I'd left the Riviera a few months ago.

One hour and a rather slow but pleasurable taxi journey later, I alighted outside Hatchards book shop in Piccadilly. Hopeful that George Henry Palmer, bookseller and publisher, could shed some much needed light on the life of Josephine Brown.

———— ◉ ————

I ENTERED THE SHOP to the sound of the tinkling bell, and immediately a tousled red head followed by a round bespectacled face popped up from behind the counter. His tall, thin build was incongruous with his cherubic like face. Gerry told me his nickname at Cambridge had been Matches. I thought it a little cruel, but in-keeping with his sunny disposition, George hadn't taken offense in the slightest.

"Ella, what a pleasant surprise," he said as he came forward to greet me. "I haven't seen you in here for a while."

"Hello, George. No, I was away for most of the summer in France."

"Ah, yes. I did hear something of that nature."

"Oh, did you?"

"It's not everyday someone you know is responsible for solving a case of international fraud. It was in all the papers. Although you weren't mentioned by name, I realised it must have been you. Well done, Ella. Was it terribly exciting?"

"And terrifying in equal measure, George. I suppose Gerry confirmed it was me?"

"He did. He's very proud of you, you know. How is Gerry, by the way? Slaving over the typewriter, I hope?"

"You may speak in jest, George, but that's precisely what he's doing. I've hardly seen him since I arrived over a week ago. He sends his regards."

"That's excellent news. He's our most popular author. A favourite of you know who," he said, inclining his head backwards.

I looked up at the Royal Warrant hung on the wall behind the desk.

"Is he really? Well, isn't that marvelous? Does Gerry know?"

"Of course, although he's not one to boast as you know. He leaves that to me," he grinned. "His Majesty has already ordered the next one."

Of course, we weren't to know it at the time, but the King would never receive Gerry's next book. A little under two months later an announcement would leave the nation, indeed the entire world, reeling with shock.-

"Now, can I offer you tea? I have a wonderful new blend from next door, all the way from Japan."

"It sounds wonderful, but perhaps next time?"

George smiled knowingly and nodded.

"Of course. Am I correct in assuming you're wearing your detective hat today, Ella?"

"Yes, I am, as a matter of fact."

"The body in the Long Water?"

"Well, either you're psychic or you've read about it in the newspaper. I'm opting for the second theory. Can I see? Our papers were late this morning."

The bell above the door tinkled once again and several new customers entered. I took a seat out of the way and read the paper while George assisted. The article was at the bottom of page three.

A Watery Grave

The body of an as yet unidentified female was found trapped under The Serpentine Bridge in Kensington Palace Gardens, in the early hours of Tuesday. It is thought she

slipped while walking on the wet bank, rendering herself un-
conscious, then fell into the Long Water where she tragically
drowned. Due to the heavy rains it is presumed her body was
washed down to the bridge where it stuck fast, before being
found by the constabulary. Police are asking for witnesses to
come forward.

The article then went on to list details and a telephone number for those who may have seen something and wished to help the police with their inquiries. I folded the newspaper and put it back on the desk just as George returned, his customers having left with several purchases.

"So, not a tragic accident then if you're on the case?"

"I'm afraid not. But I must ask you to keep that information to yourself, George. Her identity hasn't been made public yet as we need to find her family."

"My lips are sealed, Ella. How can I help?"

"This was found in the deceased's handbag," I said, handing him the bookmark. "It's one of yours, which is what led me here."

"It is, but this is from January last year. It promotes *Three Act Tragedy*, Agatha Christie's book, which was published that month." He picked up another bookmark from his desk. "See here, this is the one for this year. Promoting *Pigeon Post* by Arthur Ransome. It's the sixth in his Swallows and Amazons series."

"I don't think I've ever picked one up. I can't imagine why. Do you have new ones printed every year?"

"Yes. Sometimes twice. It all depends on what book we're promoting at the time. People like to collect them too."

"So, if she did come here then it would have been last year?"

"Either that or she received the bookmark elsewhere more recently. A friend or colleague perhaps?"

"Yes, that would make sense too. Do you keep a note of all your sales, George? She's been in her present employ for a year and a half so it's likely she came in during that time. She was a nanny at a house in Mayfair and the only book on her entire bookshelf was *The Thirty-nine Steps*."

"Well, we're not the only book shop in London, you know. Although we are the oldest. But the good news for you is we write all sales down in designated ledgers. I'll have a look from April last year, then if we don't find anything I can go back further. What was her name?"

"Miss Josephine Brown. Thank you, George. I do appreciate it."

It didn't take George long to find the correct entry. It was listed in mid-April and she did indeed purchase the John Buchan novel.

I made a note in my little book. I'd need to tell Baxter. I wasn't sure if it meant anything important but she'd purchased the tome just prior to beginning her employment with the Parfitts.

"George, do you have a copy of the book? I'd like to buy one." I doubted it would help with my inquiries but it sounded like a thrilling adventure and was one I hadn't read.

Five minutes later I left with a parcel under my arm, having thanked George profusely for his help, and went next door for more preserve for Gerry.

I HAD A SOLITARY LUNCH upon my return home, then settled in front of the fire in the drawing room to read my new book.

It had been one o'clock when I'd opened it to the first page and when the telephone rang and Betty informed me it was Baxter, it was nearly three. I couldn't believe two hours had passed in the blink of an eye. Richard Hannay was to blame of course. What an exciting life he led, and I'd been with him every step of the way. Rather reluctantly, I marked my page, then went to speak to my colleague.

"Fancy coming out for tea, Miss Bridges?"

Baxter had never invited me out for tea before, nor would I expect him to. It must be something to do with the case.

"I never say no to tea, Baxter. What's the occasion?"

"I've managed to track down Miss Brown's former employer, Dame Mildred Pocklington. We're meeting her in half an hour at Lyons Corner House on The Strand. I'll meet you outside, shall I?"

"Lyons?" I said. "Are you sure?"

There was a deafening silence.

"Yes. I even wrote it down, Miss Bridges. Why do you ask?"

His pithy tone startled me.

"Oh, Baxter, I do apologise. I didn't mean that the way it sounded. Of course you're sure. It just seems an unusual choice for a lady of her standing, that's all."

"Perhaps she likes to slum it with the masses on occasion?"

Oh dear, I really had put my foot in it. But by the same token it was most unusual for Baxter to take offense. I happened to like the Lyons establishments. They were full of genuine people having fun and the atmosphere was always vibrant. But I could hardly tell Baxter that now without sounding patronising.

"You're absolutely right, Baxter, just ignore me."

I quickly brought him up to date with what I'd learned at Hatchards, then told him I'd see him shortly.

It was too far for me to walk and be there on time, so after terminating the call with Baxter, I arranged for a taxi. I arrived at The Strand with only minutes to spare and found him waiting for me outside the tea shop. I was about to take him aside to apologise once again, when he spoke.

"I believe I owe you an apology, Miss Bridges. I was a bit curt on the telephone when all you were doing was making an observation."

"Really, Baxter, there's no need. Is there something the matter? Can I help at all?"

He shook his head. "No, there's nothing you can do. I just have a few things on my mind, that's all."

Whether it was to do with our inquiry or something of a personal nature, I couldn't be sure. But I could tell Baxter didn't want to talk. If and when the time came, I would be there to listen and help if I could, he knew that. Instead I changed the subject.

"So, what does Dame Pocklington look like?"

He shrugged. "I have no idea."

I stared at him. With seating for over two thousand people on three separate floors it would be like trying to find a black cat in a coal cellar.

He gave a little chuckle. "She'll be wearing a plumed hat with a peacock feather. She'll also be at a rear table on the first floor."

I returned Baxter's grin. "Alright, I deserved that. Well, let's see if we can find her, shall we?" I said, pushing open the door and entering a world of noise and organised chaos.

———————⬤———————

THE GROUND FLOORS OF all the Lyons establishments were given over to the shops, selling a variety of cakes, sweets, fruit and items from a delicatessen counter. The queue of people waiting to be served was already snaking to the outer door.

Baxter and I took the stairs up to the first floor, staying to one side as a variety of customers swarmed down. I glanced over my shoulder and saw just as many behind me. It certainly was a popular place.

On the first floor I observed an army of nippies in their familiar uniforms: black Alpaca dresses with a double row of pearl buttons, and starched white caps with the famous red 'L' embroidered at the front, scurrying from table to table armed with trays of tea, sandwiches and cakes.

"Table for two, sir?" a supervisor asked Baxter, his voice rising to be heard over the clatter of crockery, silver-ware and the hubbub of myriad conversations. He was a short middle-aged man in pinstriped trousers, a black jacket and bow tie around the collar of a starched white shirt. He barely came up to Baxter's shoulder.

Baxter shook his head.

"Actually, we're meeting someone."

"Oh, very good, sir. Please go through."

We maneuvered our way past full tables positioned between large marble pillars, and huge brass urns containing ferns twice as tall as Baxter. We skirted perambulators and small children with sticky hands playing on the floor and avoided wheeled trolleys full of tempting sweets, slowly making our way to the rear of the dining room. It was Baxter who saw Dame Pocklington first.

"There she is."

I glanced to a table in the far corner where I observed a stout, plain woman with a large unsightly mole on her chin, somewhere in her middle fifties at a guess, wearing a tattered fur which looked as though it had been brought out of attic storage especially for the occasion. Although this was nothing compared to the monstrosity of a hat. It was festooned to within an inch of its life with a various assortment of dusty plumage. The once vibrant colours lost to age and upon closer examination, moths. But the pièce de résistance was the enormous single peacock feather affixed to the front by a large floppy bow and diamante brooch combination. It stood straight up at least two foot, and I wondered how on earth she managed to get through a doorway without knocking the whole dreadful ensemble off.

"Ah, Baxter and Bridges, I assume?" she said, making us sound like a vaudeville act. "Have a seat."

Unfortunately, Dame Pocklington wasn't the only one waiting for us. Positioned behind her was a tall pedestal table with a dried flower arrangement. And next to that, with his purple collar and silver bell sat my cat Phantom. He gave me a brazen look with his luminous green eyes, then shot out a paw in an attempt to snag a feather from the grotesque headpiece.

I rested my forehead on my hand briefly. This could very well turn into a disaster.

"Bit of a head, have you, dear? I positively swear by Carbolic Smoke Balls. Can't beat them," the Dame said, speaking in such a way it sounded as though her cheeks were stuffed with the balls themselves. "Or Beecham's Pills. Not quite as good, but they'll do in a pinch."

"I'm quite alright, Dame Pocklington, thank you. Just a little light-headed. I'm sure tea will help."

Once our drinks had arrived, along with an assortment of finger sandwiches and cakes, I turned to Dame Pocklington.

"I do hope we've not put you to any inconvenience? We would have been more than happy to come to you."

She waved away my concerns with a much-bejewelled hand. "I had an appointment nearby, anyway. Besides, we're having a lot of work done on the townhouse at the moment and it's simply not fit for visitors."

I smiled and nodded. I decided to leave the questioning to Baxter while I studied the woman a little more closely. There was no doubt she was an eccentric but there was something else about her. Something I couldn't quite put my finger on. My thoughts weren't helped by Phantom, who hissed every time the woman opened her mouth.

"So, when did Miss Brown leave your employ?" Baxter began.

"A year and a half ago," she replied immediately, unpinning her mangy fox stole and draping it over the back of the spare chair opposite me, its glass eyes fixing me with a stare that made me shiver in revulsion. The removal of the garment had revealed a three-strand pearl necklace, tight against the thick neck. A necklace that while pretty was most assuredly a fake.

"My children are grown now, of course, but she was such a help I was loath to part with her. I had rather hoped she would be there for my grandchildren, but alas it wasn't to be. My daughter married an American and moved to New York, and my son and his wife left just before Josephine and are currently in India. It was only fair to allow her to seek other employment for which she'd been trained."

"And what of her family?"

"Well, she never mentioned a family to me. If she had one, I know nothing of them."

"And friends? Was she stepping out with anyone?"

"I'm afraid I have no knowledge of that either. I gave her one day a week and Sundays off. How she spent her time or who with I couldn't say."

"And she'd never been in any sort of trouble when in your employ? Or made any enemies that you know of?"

"Certainly not. She was a nanny, my dear man. What possible enemies could a nanny have?"

"Just one more question, then I think we can leave it there for the time being. I assume she came to you with references? Did you follow them up?"

"She came to me from a friend of a friend, so there was no need. I was perfectly happy with their assessment."

"Can I have their details?"

"Well, I'm afraid my friend died in a riding accident a long time ago. As to her friend, I don't know who it was so I can't help you there."

Baxter nodded and put away his notebook, signalling the questioning was over.

"Well, I do hope I've been of some use," Dame Pocklington said, rising and retrieving the stole. "Poor girl, such a tragedy. I do hope you find the person responsible."

And with that she left in a miasma of fusty fur with overtones of camphor.

"So, what do you make of all that?" Baxter asked me.

"I'm afraid she's lying for the most part. Hiding more than she's telling and she is not who she says she is."

"Good grief. Are you sure? I thought she sounded quite plausible myself."

"Oh, I agree she was very good. But her outfit was a mockery and years out of date. Apart from looking as though it came from an old dressing-up box or the local theatre. Her jewellery, although quite well done, was paste. And don't get me started on her shoes."

"I see. I must be losing my touch," he said a little irritably. "Anything else?"

"Yes, as a matter of fact. Her hands. That woman has done her fair share of manual labour, and quite recently I should say. Her entire ridiculous ensemble and eccentric persona was an attempt to misdirect us, Baxter. I stand by my analysis. She's hiding something. The question is what and why?"

<hr />

BY THE TIME I ARRIVED home I really was feeling out of sorts. My head throbbed with a combination of the heavy odors emanating from the imitation Dame, and the constant noise level at the Lyons tea house. I was also worried about Baxter. He'd seemed particularly dejected at his inability to see Mildred Pocklington for what she really was.

I'd just divested myself of coat and hat when Gerry came out of the library.

"Hello, Ella, I thought I heard the door. I say, are you alright? You look a little peaky."

"Just a bit of a headache coming on. I think I'll take supper to my room and have an early night. But first, do you have a copy of Who's Who about?"

"Yes, in the library. Come on, I'll get it for you."

I followed Gerry into the heated room where there was a welcome fire blazing in the grate and warmed myself while he found the latest volume.

"Here you are. What are you looking for?"

"A Dame Mildred Pocklington, or her husband." I searched the P's but found no reference to either a Sir, or a Baronet, nor the lady herself. I was right, she didn't exist.

"Thank you, Gerry."

"You're welcome, Ella. Go and get some rest, I'll see that Betty brings up your supper later. Do you want something now? Tea perhaps?"

"No, thank you, Gerry. I've had enough tea for today."

I was halfway up the stairs when Gerry called me back.

"Oh, I nearly forgot. Aunt Margaret telephoned while you were out. She's coming to stay for a while. She'll be here around mid-morning tomorrow."

"Oh, that's wonderful news."

"Thought it might cheer you up. Good night, Ella."

"Good night, Gerry. See you in the morning."

I ascended the stairs feeling much lighter of heart and much relieved. My aunt and I got on very well and had worked together on a couple of cases. One at the village fete on Linhay and the most recent in the Riviera, along with her friend and former colleague Pierre, a well-known artist who also happened to be a dwarf.

She'd led a very interesting life thus far and although she hadn't said anything to me outright, she'd intimated more than once to being part of a clandestine organisation working on behalf of the British Government abroad.

I took her visit to be a very good omen. Perhaps she could help me make sense of my current inquiry because so far it was mystery piled upon mystery.

Chapter Five

AT ELEVEN O'CLOCK ON the dot the next morning, a taxi pulled up outside the house and my Aunt Margaret alighted. She must have risen at the crack of dawn to arrive all the way from Sheffield as early as she had.

"Aunt Margaret," I cried and skipped down the steps to greet her. "What a wonderful surprise. I'm so glad you're here."

I must have sounded more relieved than I'd meant to, for my aunt held me at arms' length and looked at me sharply.

"What on earth has happened, Ella? You don't look at all well."

"I'm fine, Aunt, don't worry. It's just Baxter and I are working on a new case which is proving a tad baffling. Plus, I think there's something the matter with him."

"With Baxter?"

"Yes, he's not himself at all and I'm worried about him. Look, I'll tell you all about it when we get inside."

While we had been talking Gerry had paid off the taxi driver, eschewing his offer to carry my aunt's belongings inside, and was lugging the suitcases up the steps himself.

"Gerry, my dear boy," Aunt Margaret said in greeting, as we finally shut the door on the damp weather and stood in the hallway.

"Aunt Margaret, welcome. It's very good to see you."

"Give an old lady a hug, dear."

I scoffed. "Old lady? Hardly."

"Very good of you to say so, Ella," my aunt said with a grin, as she released Gerry and began to remove her hat.

"You were fishing for a compliment. I should have known."

"Of course, dear. They don't come as often as they used to. Now, where's the lovely Virginia?"

Ginny was waiting in the drawing room with elevenses.

"Aunt Margaret, how lovely to see you," she said, struggling slightly to get out of her armchair.

My aunt kissed her on both cheeks and told her how wonderful she looked. "A picture of health, my dear."

"Tea, Aunt?" Ginny asked once she'd resumed her seat.

"Coffee for me, darling. It's been a rather long journey."

"Did you get the train, then?" I asked.

"I did. Kings Cross was awash with people and the taxi took an age to get here. The storm did a fair bit of damage to our capital, I see?"

"Yes. I barely missed being caught in it myself. Although there's been a huge amount of work done on clearing things up already. The army was drafted in to help," I explained. "Why didn't your driver bring you?"

"It's time I gave the poor man some proper time off. Besides, I didn't know how long I would be staying."

"You're welcome to stay as long as you like, Aunt Margaret," Gerry said, helping himself to another biscuit.

"I know that, dear, thank you. But I'm not one for outstaying my welcome as you know. However, I have decided a change is in order and to that end I'm also here to purchase a house."

"You're moving to London?"

"I am."

"Oh, but that's fabulous news. You'll be so much nearer to us all," I said.

"Which is precisely my reason for moving, Ella. Regardless of the joke in the hall, I'm not getting any younger and with a new addition to the family imminent, I find I'd like to spend more time with my family. And before you ask, no, I am not ill."

My aunt knew me well for this is immediately what had I thought. It was a relief to be told otherwise. We continued to discuss possible locations for her new home, then moved onto news from other members of the family, before Ginny and Gerry both made their excuses and left my aunt and me alone.

"So, Ella. What is this new case you have? I'd like to help if I can."

"WELL, IT ALL STARTED when I found a baby abandoned in the park on Monday..."

I recounted my shock and subsequent dash home with the pram in order to miss the impending storm. My telephone call to Baxter and his finding of the parents, resulting in them being reunited.

"Unfortunately, the next day the body of the child's nanny was discovered under the bridge."

I continued by explaining what we'd done thus far, culminating in the interview of the woman posing as Dame Mildred Pocklington.

"So, there were only two things of particular interest in the nanny's handbag: the bookmark and the curious note?" my aunt asked.

"Yes. Although the bookmark turned out to be of little consequence. According to George Palmer she bought a copy of *The Thirty-nine Steps* in April last year. I obtained a copy myself, but apart from it being a ripping good yarn I can't see it being an important part of the investigation."

"Perhaps it's the nanny's copy that's important, Ella, rather than the story."

"What a fool I've been! Of course, why didn't I think of that? I'll visit the Parfitts later and ask to borrow it."

Aunt Margaret retrieved her spectacles from her bag and after putting them on, held out her hand. "Let me see the note. If it was hidden in the lining of the bag as you say, it most likely means something."

"The original is still with Baxter at The Yard, but I copied it out exactly. Here."

I handed her my notebook, and she tore a piece of paper from her writing pad and copied out her own version.

"Utter nonsense, isn't it?"

"At first glance."

"And second and third," I said morosely. "Baxter and I tried for ages."

"Don't be so defeatist, Ella. We'll work it out, eventually. Now, why don't you ring for more coffee? This has gone cold."

I got up and went over to the bell pull.

"Oh! For goodness sake, Ella, really I... oh, you're over there. I apologise. I take it this wasn't your fault then?"

I looked at the dregs of the cold coffee spilled over my aunt's note. Then at Phantom who was sitting on the table licking his paw and looking very pleased with himself.

"No, it wasn't me."

"Your invisible cat?"

"I'm afraid so. Although to be fair to him, he rarely does anything like this without a good reason."

"I believe you, Ella. It seems he had a good reason this time too."

"REALLY? LET ME SEE."

I looked at the coffee stained paper and was amazed to see the word 'nil' hidden in 'manille.'

"Nil. So what does it mean, nothing? Or none perhaps?"

"Have a closer look, Ella."

I looked at the rest of the words.

"There's a number nine in 'puniness!' This probably means 'nil' is for zero. Oh, well done, Phantom."

He looked at me, turned, then bounded majestically up from the table to the windowsill where he proceeded to walk through the solid glass. I was always mesmerised by his ability to do this. He seemed to exist in several realities at once. Perhaps wherever he was at that moment it was the height of summer and the window had been open. Unfortunately, I was stuck in a time and place where the rain was coming down in torrents and lashing noisily against the pane. I turned back to my aunt.

"So, what do you think it is? A bank account number maybe? or possibly a map reference?"

"It could be any number of things, Ella. We'll need to work out the rest of it to be certain."

At that moment we were interrupted by Betty saying lunch was served in the dining room.

"We'll come back to it later, Ella. I suggest while I continue to direct my vast mental capacity to working it out, you go to the Parfitts and collect the nanny's book. It could have something to do with it."

"Oh, a certain page number or chapters or something like that? Good thinking, Aunt Margaret."

"Thank you, dear."

"Do you think it might look a little strange if I turn up asking for just the book? The rest of her belongings are also there and I suppose in the absence of a next-of-kin we really should remove everything."

"Well, what's stopping you?"

"Baxter, I suppose. I don't want to upset him anymore than I appear to have done. Although it was entirely unintentional. I think I'll telephone him after lunch and update him."

"Good thinking, Ella."

I laughed. "Thank you, dear."

Lunch was poached salmon, buttered potatoes and carrots julienne. Followed by peaches and cream. But I confess I hardly tasted any of it. An hour later I was dressed for our inclement weather and eager to get to James and Elizabeth Parfitt's Mayfair home. I did however telephone first to make sure it was convenient and to ask that Miss Brown's belongings were packed as I was coming to collect them. I telephoned The Yard and asked to speak to Baxter, but he was unavailable so I left a message with a constable explaining what I was doing and asked him to relay the information to my colleague. I also organised a taxi.

The journey took no more than a quarter of an hour and I watched the clean-up process going on in the gardens as we drove down Bayswater Road. With the body of Josephine Brown removed and the police having completed their search for clues, the park was once again open to the public. Although with the current rain there wasn't a soul in sight.

I asked the taxi driver to wait for me and before I had reached the door, it was opened. Once again the butler asked me to remain in the drawing room while he fetched Elizabeth Parfitt.

"Miss Bridges, how nice to see you again."

"Mrs Parfitt, thank you for accommodating my request so quickly. I hope it wasn't too short notice?"

"Please, do call me Elizabeth and no it wasn't inconvenient in the slightest. It was a relatively quick job as she didn't have much in the way of personal items. To be honest, I'm rather relieved to be able to clear the rooms. Forgive me, I don't mean to sound selfish. What happened to her was terribly distressing. I've been quite heart-sick about it. But I've been unable to seek a replacement while her belongings were still here. Their continued presence was beginning to make me feel uncomfortable too. Does that sound quite terrible?"

I shook my head. "Not at all. I fully understand, Elizabeth. It's a perfectly normal response and hopefully you'll begin to feel a little better now they are to be removed. And rest assured, Baxter and I will find the miscreant responsible."

Elizabeth Parfitt grasped my hands. "Thank you for understanding and for listening. James refuses to talk about it. I think it's upset him terribly, but he's managing to keep a stiff upper lip. Now, I believe my Butler has what you came for."

We ventured back into the hall where the Parfitt's butler was stowing two suitcases into the boot of the motor car, and just before I got in, I saw the spirit of Josephine Brown watching me from across the road, Phantom sitting at her feet. I gave her a smile and a quick nod to let her know I was investigating what had happened to her.

Barely an hour after I'd left, I was back at Brunswick Gardens. Betty opened the door for me.

"Be a dear, would you, Betty, and bring in the luggage?"

"Yes, miss. Been shopping have you, miss?" Then she caught sight of the battered suitcases and screwed up her nose. "Expectin' someone else are we, miss?"

"No. No one else, Betty."

By the time I had hung up my coat and hat, Betty had deposited the two suitcases and two hatboxes in the hall and disappeared back to the kitchen to arrange our tea. I found the book on the top inside the first suitcase and returned to the drawing room and my aunt.

"I've got it, Aunt Margaret."

"Jolly good, Ella. I believe I've got it too."

<hr/>

"YOU HAVE? SHOW ME WHAT you've done."

Once Aunt Margaret had extracted the numbers from the nonsensical passage, and we had replaced the word nil with the numeral zero, we were left with the following numbers: 0204309. Or possibly 020 4309.

"Good heavens, Aunt Margaret. Could that be a telephone number? I don't know of a 020 prefix but I can't think what else it could be. At the very least, I should try it and see, just in case."

"Well, you might want to wait..."

"No, if it is a telephone number then we need to know who it belongs to as soon as possible. It could be important," I replied dashing to the door just as Betty came in with the tea tray.

"But, Ella, there's..."
"Don't worry, Aunt Margaret, I won't be long."
"As you wish, dear."

I was astonished to find it was indeed a telephone number and was answered by a dignified and slightly haughty male voice.

"Noble and Vaughn, good afternoon."

Now where had I seen that name before? I wracked my brains for a moment and suddenly remembered it was a gentleman's tailor on Jermyn Street. It's where Gerry got his shirts.

"Er, hello," I stammered. Not actually expecting it to be a telephone number, I really hadn't thought through what I was going to say. I decided to disguise my voice a little, make it slightly rougher and pretend to be in the same line of work as Josephine Brown who was the link.

"Yes, um, I'm a nanny."

There was a distinct pause then, "Congratulations, madam."

"Yes, thank you. Er, do you have many nannies coming into your establishment?"

"Not as a rule, madam. We're a gentleman's bespoke outfitters."

I blinked.

"Well, a friend of mine, another nanny actually, gave me your number."

"Perhaps she telephoned on behalf of her employer, Madam?" he said in slow tones as though I were dimwitted. I could hardly blame him for thinking so, considering my dismal performance.

"Yes, that might have been the case. Can you tell me if you have Mr Parfitt as a customer?"

"No, madam."

"No, you don't or no, you can't tell me?"

"Definitely one or the other, madam. Would you like to reserve an appointment for a *gentleman*?"

"Not at the moment, thank you. But I'll telephone again and let you know."

"I'll look forward to it, madam," he said. Then he hung up.

I stared at the receiver for a moment before hanging up myself and returning to my aunt, who was doubled over with laughter.

———— ◉ ————

"WENT WELL, DID IT, dear?" she asked, once she'd come up for air.

"You know very well it didn't."

"Well, I did try to stop you."

"Not terribly hard."

"Short of tackling you to the floor there wasn't much I could do."

"Well anyway," I said, taking a sandwich from the plate on the table and throwing myself in a chair. "It was a complete waste of time."

"To whom did the number belong?"

"Noble and Vaughn. A Jermyn Street gentleman's outfitters. I tried to find out if James Parfitt was a customer but he wouldn't tell me. Not that it would have made any difference. Besides, I'd already noticed he was a Savile Row man. It's a complete dead end."

"I wouldn't be too sure about that, Ella. I've managed to decipher the remainder of the note."

"What? I thought the number was it."

"No, dear. The letters that remain once you've removed the numbers actually make up a sentence. It's quite clever, actually."

I looked at what my aunt had done:

*'A ma**nille** **two**folds a tin**nily** **four**square.*
__Three__some, se__niles__, pu__niness__'
'A male folds a tiny square.
Some sees puss.'

"I thought the number was odd, but that doesn't make any sense either."

"It doesn't need to, dear. That's the whole point of a secret communication. The more obscure the better in fact, so you know you're speaking with the right person. It is obviously a code of some sort or why bother to hide it in such a clever way?"

"We need to visit the shop, don't we?"

"Yes, I think we do."

I glanced at the clock on the mantelpiece, just after five.

"Let me go and speak to Gerry."

I walked down the hall and listened at the library door. The typewriter was silent which was a good sign. I knocked and opened the door slightly. Gerry was at his desk going through a manuscript.

"Hello, Ella. Everything alright?"

"Yes. Just a quick question. Do you know what time Noble and Vaughn close?"

"Half-past five. Why? Are you thinking of getting me a shirt?"

"I think you have enough shirts, Gerry. No, it's just come up as part of the case. Not to worry. Thank you."

I returned to the drawing room.

"We're too late for today I'm afraid. The shop closes in twenty minutes. We'd never get there in time."

"We'll go tomorrow, Ella. I'm sure it will still be there in the morning. In the meantime, we can have a look at Miss Brown's book. There may be something of interest there too."

Chapter Six

AT TEN O'CLOCK THE next morning Aunt Margaret and I jumped in a taxi and directed the driver to Jermyn Street. I had no idea what to expect when we got there, but suffice to say it was one of the strangest episodes of my career.

The previous evening we had worked our way through Josephine Brown's copy of *The Thirty-Nine Steps*, but except for numerous notations and a hand-written list of nursery rhymes in the front, which I assumed the nanny was teaching her young charge, we found nothing of import.

Baxter had sent a constable to pick up the nanny's belongings and take them back to Scotland Yard, all but the book which I decided to keep for the time being. He also returned Rupert's perambulator to his parents. I wrote Baxter a note explaining that we'd broken the code, and we were going to follow it up the next morning. I asked the constable to pass it on as a matter of urgency.

Just over half an hour later we alighted the taxi on the opposite side of the road to Noble and Vaughn's, giving us time to study the comings and goings. Luckily the weather was clear and bright with no sign of rain. Although there was a cold snap in the air.

We huddled in a shop doorway with a clear line of sight to the tailor's and waited.

"So, we just march in there, spout this nonsense sentence and hope something happens which doesn't include us being carted off to the nearest asylum?" I said.

Aunt Margaret laughed. "Yes, that's about the measure of it. But don't worry if it does, I'm a dab hand at getting out of a strait-jacket."

"I have no idea how to respond to that little gem, Aunt. Look, there's someone exiting the shop. Wait, I know her. It's the woman Baxter and I interviewed at Lyons. The one pretending to be Dame Pocklington. Although she's plainly dressed today and sans the ghastly hat. I knew she was a fraud."

"Do you want to follow her?"

"I most certainly do," I said, starting after her only to see her jump on a bus a moment later. "Oh, well. Back to plan A."

We entered the shop to the greeting of a bell and came face to face with a dapper-looking gentleman with hooded eyes and an aquiline nose.

"Good morning, ladies. May I be of assistance?"

I immediately recognised the voice of the man I'd spoken to on the telephone and cringed.

"You possibly can, young man," my aunt replied, slowly perusing the garments. She spied a display of silk handkerchiefs and wandered over, lifting a magenta one that had been cleverly folded into the shape of a swan.

"Your work, Mr...?"

"Pitkin, Madam. Yes, indeed."

"A male folds a tiny square," my aunt said.

He looked at her for a moment, then looked at me. Then my aunt looked at me. Right, I thought, here's goes nothing and said brightly, "Some sees puss," like a deranged simpleton.

Honestly, you could have knocked me down with a feather at what happened next.

The shopkeeper gave us a curt bow, closed and locked the door, then extracted two keys from a small drawer underneath the till.

"Please, follow me."

I looked at my aunt in astonishment.

"Close your mouth, Ella, or you'll give the game away before it's started," she whispered in amusement.

We followed him through to a back room where I spied a second telephone. I'd already spotted the one in the main shop. So they had two telephone lines, how curious. At least it explained the odd prefix I had dialed the day before. Pitkin opened a door and led us down a steep flight of curved stone steps. There must have been at least forty and my legs were aching by the time we'd reached the cellar floor. At the far side he unlocked another door and opened it to reveal a tunnel. I swallowed a gasp. What on earth had we got ourselves into this time?

———◉———

MR PITKIN HANDED AUNT Margaret a key with the head in the shape of a cat. I imagined Phantom chuckling at the irony.

"Follow the tunnel until you find the door this unlocks."

"How will we recognise it, Pitkin?"

"You'll know it when you see it, Madam. It will take you approximately twenty minutes."

And with that we were ushered inside and he closed the door behind us. I heard the lock click into place. We were trapped.

"Well, there's no going back now. Come along, Ella, let's see where this takes us."

The tunnel was illuminated from above by a series of bare bulbs at intervals of fifteen feet or so, which was perfectly adequate to see our way. Underfoot the floor was of solid construction, cement most likely, while the older curved walls and ceilings were brick. It was a continuous archway approximately twelve feet high and six or seven feet across. Surprisingly, while on the cool side, there wasn't a trace of the subterranean damp I had expected.

We walked for about ten minutes, halfway there if Pitkin was to be believed, before either of us spoke.

"Where do you suppose we are, Aunt Margaret?"

"I believe, assuming my sense of direction hasn't deserted me, we're underneath St. James' Park."

I shuddered at the thought of hundreds of tonnes of earth above me and began to speed up.

"Don't worry, Ella, we're perfectly safe. Judging by the building work this tunnel has been here a very long time. There's no reason to suspect it will suddenly cave in just because we're traversing through it."

I know she meant well but oddly her words didn't reassure me one iota.

Eventually we came to a solid steel door in the right-hand side wall. At the very bottom was a small stencil in the shape of a mouse.

"This must be it," Aunt Margaret said.

"You know, that shopkeeper could quite easily have told us it would be the first door we came to rather than being so cryptic."

"Mmm."

"What is it?"

"Nothing. Let's get this over with, shall we?"

She inserted the key into the lock and turned it. With a resounding click the door swung open to reveal...

"A broom cupboard?" I said.

The space was the size of an alcove with a mop and bucket leaning against a wall and two brooms and several dusters on a shelf to the right. The lot of which looked as though they hadn't cleaned anything in years. On the back wall was another set of shelves, all empty. On the left wall was a round electric bell, and a taped set of instructions beneath.

IN ORDER
1) Lock the door
2) Ring the bell

"I feel just like Alice," I said. "All we need now is the white rabbit."

"You may get your wish sooner than you think."

"What do you mean?"

"Just ring the bell, Ella," my aunt sighed in tones of resignation, locking the door.

I did as she asked and a moment later the back wall, shelves and all, swung outward to reveal a willowy young man in shirt-sleeves with a mop of blond hair and chalky skin.

"Come on through," he said.

We entered a corridor and after the man had closed the shelved door, he told us to follow. I glanced at my aunt, hoping to see her looking as puzzled as I was, but she stared straight ahead, her jaw set tight.

At the end of the corridor the man opened a door and led us into a busy office. I stood and stared. This was the last thing I had expected. Men and women were working at various desks in the utilitarian space. Telephones were ringing and world maps on the wall were covered in small pins and flags. Above the maps was a row of clocks showing the time in different cities of the world. The general buzz of energy and drama was almost overwhelming after the silence of the tunnel.

"Aunt Margaret, where on earth are we?" I whispered and turned to face her.

She gave a deep sigh. "Welcome to the Secret Intelligence Service, Ella."

I DIDN'T HAVE TIME to react to her monumental statement before a large florid man with white hair swept back from a wide forehead, charged through the door and staggered to halt, staring at my aunt in amazement.

"Snow White!"

Suddenly the atmosphere in the office changed. There was a split second of utter silence before gasps of awe and shock rippled around the room. I looked at the sea of wide-eyed faces before turning to my aunt.

"In certain circles my name is revered," she whispered. "Of course, in others it's mud. But that's by the by."

She turned back to the large man who was slowly walking towards us, utterly dumbstruck.

"Hello, Bunny."

Well, that explained her earlier white rabbit quip.

"Snow White," he said again. "I can't believe my eyes. I thought you'd retired?"

"I thought so too. This is my niece, Ella."

He turned to look at me in puzzlement. I do believe he was seeing me for the first time. Such was his shock at seeing my aunt I don't think he'd realised until that very moment she wasn't alone. Abruptly he became aware of the animated whispers surrounding us.

"I think we'd better move this into my office. Your reputation precedes you," he said. Then barked out, "Back to work, everyone."

It suddenly occurred to me I'd been looking at things the wrong way round. I'd been focused on Mildred Pocklington not being a Dame. What if the truth was Josephine Brown wasn't a nanny?

In Bunny's office, my aunt and I both took a seat while he barked out an order for tea. It seemed to me he was unable to issue an order at a more reasonable decibel level. I turned to my aunt with a raised eyebrow.

"Snow White?"

"It was my code name, dear."

"I gathered as much. Oh, wait a moment. Was this when you were working with Pierre?"

"Yes."

"Pierre your friend, who also happens to be a dwarf?"

"Indeed."

I burst out laughing, "Oh, that's just too much. I suppose it was your idea?"

"Of course. I don't think he ever forgave me."

At that point, Bunny entered and sat down opposite us.

"Poor Pierre," I said wiping my eyes.

"You're still in touch with old Grumpy, then?" Bunny asked my aunt.

And that of course set me off again, as it did Aunt Margaret. Bunny just stared and waited while we gathered ourselves together. Then he cleared his throat as the tea was brought in and left on the desk.

"Right, when you've quite finished, do you mind telling me what you're doing here? And more to the point, how you found us?"

"Of course, apologies, Bunny. Ella's with The Yard. I'm sorry to have to tell you but I believe you've lost one of your agents."

<hr />

"WHAT? WHO? HOW?" THE poor man spluttered in wide-eyed shock.

"Josephine Brown," I said. "She was murdered at some point on Monday afternoon and her body found on Tuesday morning. My colleague Detective Sergeant Baxter and I are investigating. I am sorry."

Bunny suddenly launched himself from his chair and went to the door, yelling for someone called Carstairs. It was the young man who'd collected us from the broom cupboard. There followed a brief and urgently whispered conversation, then Carstairs dashed to the nearest telephone and Bunny returned to us.

"Has she signed?" he asked my aunt.

"Signed what?" I said.

"The act! The Official Secrets Act. Have you signed it?"

"There's no need to shout at me. I'm sitting barely five feet away."

He narrowed his eyes momentarily, then glanced at Aunt Margaret with a smirk.

"Chip Off the Old Block I see. I apologise. Nightingale's loss has been a shock."

Nightingale had obviously been Josephine Brown's code name.

"So, have you?" he asked again.

"Yes, as a matter of fact I have. Lord Carrick insisted upon it."

I didn't tell him under what circumstances; it was none of his business, but my aunt suddenly took my hand.

"Oh, Ella, I'm so sorry, I never thought. This must be difficult for you. Are you alright, darling?"

"I'm fine, Aunt Margaret, don't worry. It was a long time ago."

"The Home Secretary?" Bunny said. "Wait a minute... good God, you're John's wife?"

"Widow. You knew him? Did he work for you?"

Bunny shook his head. "No. Different department, but he was a good man. A very good man. Brave. I'm sorry for your loss Mrs Wa..."

"I go by the name of Bridges now," I interrupted. "My maiden name."

"Yes, of course."

"Is everything to your satisfaction now, Bunny?" Aunt Margaret said.

"It is. But look, before we go any further, can you explain how you found us? We're the Secret Intelligence Service, for heaven's sake. The emphasis being on the *secret* part. Yet here you are. I can't have all and sundry wandering in and surprising us."

"We're not just anybody, Bunny. Ella's a consultant with Scotland Yard and has several solved cases under her belt. One recent high-profile international fraud investigation as it happens. And I'm a former agent. We therefore have skills your average British subjects don't. I doubt you'll be inundated with the masses any time soon."

Then as if to make a mockery of everything my aunt just said Carstairs came in.

"Sorry to bother you, sir, but Pitkin's on the line. There's a gentleman in the shop refusing to leave until he gets answers. Name of Baxter, sir. From Scotland Yard."

Chapter Seven

BUNNY THREW UP HIS hands in mock despair. "Oh, well isn't this just fine and dandy? Here's an idea, why not invite the whole of the London constabulary down here, shall we? Have a party?"

Carstairs was obviously used to outbursts from his superior, although admittedly he looked particularly nonplussed at this one, for he waited patiently for Bunny to calm down before asking what he should tell Pitkin.

Bunny looked at me. "You told him, I suppose?"

"Naturally I did. He's my colleague and we're working on the same case. It was before I knew of your involvement of course."

"Baxter can be trusted," Aunt Margaret added. "I've worked with him before, too."

"Alright, but he'll definitely need to sign the paperwork. Carstairs, get it ready and tell Pitkin to take him to the tunnel. Someone will meet him at the door."

"Yes, sir."

Just short of twenty minutes later I was leading Baxter through the broom cupboard and into the main office. He looked around in stunned amazement.

"What on earth is all this? Ah, now I see."

I looked to where Aunt Margaret held his gaze from the other side of the room.

"What do you mean, Baxter?"

"Things always get more complicated when you two are together, Miss Bridges."

He was right of course.

"So, you deciphered the note. I assume we've stumbled into a Secret Service case?"

"I'm afraid so, Baxter. Incredible as it sounds, it appears Josephine Brown was actually a Secret Intelligence Service agent. Look, let me introduce you to Bunny, the chap in charge, but be warned he has a short fuse and is insufferably rude."

"Sounds like a real charmer, Miss Bridges."

I laughed. "Aunt Margaret assures me his bark his worse than his bite."

"Oh, knows him well, does she?"

"I believe she used to work for him. Don't look at me like that, Baxter, I was as shocked as you are. Well, perhaps not quite that much; she's always intimated she'd had a secret life before retiring. Still, it was a bit of a surprise when it was all confirmed."

I took Baxter through to Bunny's office where I made the introductions.

"Have a seat, Baxter. I'll need you to sign this before we go any further," Bunny said, sliding the official documentation across the desk.

After several minutes of perusing the paperwork, Baxter took a pen from his inside pocket and signed and dated The Official Secrets Act. He slid it back across the desk to Bunny who promptly held it out to Carstairs to take away and, I assumed, file somewhere safe.

"Now, just so we're all on the same page, you do realise that anything we do here trumps what The Yard does? We play a long game of cat and mouse and we don't want the plod ruining what can be years of hard and important work. All of which is designed to keep the country secure."

That explained the symbolism I thought as I listened to Bunny's lecture, but I was appalled at his tone and his demeaning use of the word 'plod.' The man was sorely lacking in manners and a quick glance at Baxter told me he felt the same way.

"I wasn't aware The Yard, and the SIS worked together," he said.

"You'd be surprised," Bunny replied. "Although we don't normally work with someone at the lower levels."

I saw Baxter bristle, and I did the same on his behalf. Baxter's promotion to Detective Sergeant had been quite recent, and he'd worked and fought hard for it. He deserved it too, he was an excellent policeman and very intuitive. He held his tongue, but I saw his jaw clench. Bunny continued, seemingly oblivious, but I knew better. He was deliberately goading Baxter and by extension insulting me, but to what end I couldn't fathom.

"Usually we have contact far higher up the chain and the relevant details are filtered down on a need to know basis."

"Well, this is still my case. I have a body in the morgue..."

"No, I'm afraid you don't. And let's get one thing straight, this is no longer your case."

"Bunny."

There was a hard edge to my aunt's voice. It was a warning and I think Bunny heard it too.

"Ella, Baxter, would you mind leaving us for a moment?" she said, without taking her eyes off her former colleague.

"Are you sure, Aunt Margaret?"

"Yes, dear. This won't take long."

Baxter and I left and moved part way up the hall outside to wait, and to keep out of the way of the hustle and bustle of the main office.

"I think you oversold his charm, Miss Bridges," Baxter said, leaning against a wall with his arms crossed.

"Oh, Baxter, I'm dreadfully sorry."

"It's hardly your fault."

"I know, but I feel awful just the same. Gosh, that was just terrible wasn't it? I've never met such a bombastic and dislikable person in all my life. With such a deplorable attitude and obnoxious personality, I'm shocked he's risen to the level he has."

"You're not usually one to mince your words, Miss Bridges."

I laughed. "Yes, perhaps I was a bit harsh. But really, Baxter, perhaps we should forget all about this case. Let the Intelligence Service deal with it. Josephine Brown was one of theirs after all."

Baxter eyed me for a moment, then shook his head. "If it's all the same to you I'd rather see it through. It's still our case as far as I'm concerned." He paused for a moment, "I'd like to solve this one, Miss Bridges. If you're still willing?"

There was something in his voice that caught me unawares. It was just an impression, but it was as though the words he was saying didn't quite match the feeling behind them. There was an aura of acceptance and inevitability. Or perhaps finality. I didn't have time to analyse it properly as Carstairs came to tell us we were wanted back in Bunny's office.

I nodded in answer to Baxter's question. "Yes, of course I'm amenable. You're right, it's still our case and we have a duty to Miss Brown to see it through."

———◉———

THE BUNNY WHO WAS SITTING in the office this time round was a different version to the one we'd met previously. I had no idea what my aunt had said to him but whatever it was had worked. He was still gruff but not deliberately rude.

"Right, where were we?"

"You were explaining how we had neither a body nor a case," Baxter said.

Bunny winced. "Yes. Look, Nightingale was one of ours and we look after our own. As you've no doubt surmised, Josephine Brown wasn't her real name." He held up a hand. "Before you ask, I can't tell you what it was. She's being taken back to her family. They've been informed."

"Baxter and I were talking in the hall," I said. "We would like to continue working on the case. With you. We are not the enemy and we have skills and experience we can bring to the investigation that will help find whoever is responsible. We feel we owe Miss Brown that much."

Bunny glanced quickly at my aunt then back at us. "Yes, alright. But first can you please tell me how the devil you found us? If there's a hole in our security, I need to find it and block it up."

I took a deep breath and began to tell my story for what seemed like the one hundredth time. But I'd barely got further than finding the baby abandoned before Bunny interrupted.

"Wait! You say Rupert Parfitt was hidden and abandoned in Kensington gardens?"

"That's right."

"Is something the matter, Bunny?" Aunt Margaret asked.

"Yes, there could well be. This might not be what I thought it was." He turned back to me. "We'll come back to it in a minute. Carry on, Miss Bridges."

"Well, in all honesty it's very simple. Baxter and I found a coded note hidden in the lining of Miss Brown's handbag. We couldn't make head nor tail of it but I showed it to Aunt Margaret when she arrived and she solved it. I telephoned the number contained therein and found it belonged to Noble and Vaughn. We arrived here today having also worked out the coded sentence, which we gave to your man Pitkin, and here we are."

"Could Miss Brown's murder have been the result of a mugging gone awry?" he asked.

I thought not, but I looked at Baxter to answer.

"No, I don't think so. She was attacked from behind. It was calculated and I believe she was the deliberate target. Besides, we found her handbag intact. Her purse contained coins, and she was still wearing her watch. There wasn't even an attempt to make it look like a robbery."

"Why do you ask, Bunny?" Aunt Margaret said.

"Because Nightingale was placed at the Parfitt residence to report back on James. I had thought perhaps he'd discovered her duplicity and done away with her, but no father would abandon his child as Miss Bridges just described. We may very well be looking for a third party."

"Why was she reporting on James Parfitt?" I asked, leaning forward expectantly. I felt something extraordinary was about to be shared. Perhaps my initial dislike of Nightingale's employer wasn't unwarranted after all.

"Because, Miss Bridges, James Parfitt is almost certainly a Russian spy."

———⬤———

IT WAS WITH UTTER RELIEF I found myself back outside in natural daylight just over half an hour after Bunny's astonishing announcement. I took several deep breaths, even enjoying the feeling of slight drizzle on my face and turned to Baxter and my aunt.

"I don't know how people are able to work in such an oppressive atmosphere. No windows and so far below the surface. I think I'd go quite mad without being able to see the sky."

"Take it from me, it's much more difficult to cope with when you know you can't get out," Aunt Margaret said enigmatically. "Now, it would appear we missed tea and I for one am famished. What say both of you? Shall we partake, somewhere light and airy?"

"Thank you, but not for me. Mrs Baxter'll have my guts for garters if I'm late again. Besides, if I'm honest, there's nothing that can beat my wife's cooking. I daresay we'll be in touch one way or another if you need me, Miss Bridges."

"Of course, Baxter. I expect Bunny will get together a suitable plan shortly."

He tipped his hat then my Aunt Margaret, and I watched him shamble off in the direction of The Yard.

"You're right Ella, he's not quite himself, is he?"

Aunt Margaret hailed a taxi for us and instructed the driver to take us to The Dorchester, their afternoon tea in the Park Lounge being one of the best in the city.

Once we were settled by a window, I asked my aunt the obvious question.

"So, what did you say to Bunny to cause such a remarkable change in his disposition?"

"I've known Bunny long enough to see he was over-compensating."

"In what way?"

"It was quite obvious to me the poor man was in pain. All the bravado and bluster, and yes the insults, were masking something else. You see, one of the reactions to both fear and guilt is anger."

"I'm afraid I don't understand what you're trying to say, Aunt Margaret."

"Personal relationships within the agency are frowned upon. Actively discouraged actually and for good reason. Families are a liability I'm sad to say as they can be used against you. You of all people would know that better than most."

Stupidly, I still hadn't put two and two together, but I knew if I stayed silent my aunt would eventually explain. And she did.

"This undercover assignment was to be Josephine Brown's last. She was due to retire from active duty and take a supporting office-based role. It's what she wanted. She knew she'd never be free to marry and have some semblance of a normal life otherwise."

"Go on."

"The man Josephine was going to marry was Bunny. We didn't just shock him with the news one of his agents had been killed, but his fiancé."

———◆◆———

AS YOU CAN IMAGINE, I felt absolutely dreadful at this news. I'd called Bunny some choice names, feeling at the time they'd been warranted. Now, knowing he'd been struggling to keep his grief at bay and secret from his subordinates, who were unaware of his true relationship with Nightingale, my guilt was almost overwhelming. I said as much to my aunt.

"There's no need to feel guilty, Ella. Bunny, regardless of his reasons, was at fault for his attitude. It was unprofessional. He admitted as much and asked me to relay his apologies. His natural personality is gruff and overbearing at times but he is a good man, Ella. His job is very difficult as you can imagine, with the welfare of so many undercover operatives being his ultimate responsibility. He blames himself entirely for what happened to Josephine. Being unable to protect the person he loved and was planning to build a future with will haunt him for the rest of his days. But he is more determined than ever to find out who was responsible. He'll never let it go, Ella, and he'll never be able to begin the process of grieving properly and healing until it's solved. I would like to help him."

"Of course. I would too. I think the best place to start would be with the fact the Secret Intelligence Service believes James Parfitt is a spy for the Russians."

Working for the Foreign Office, James Parfitt was well placed to pass on sensitive government information. He'd obviously been under scrutiny for a while if Nightingale's year and a half placement was any indication. But had he in fact killed her because she'd finally found proof of his treachery? Before she had a chance to pass it on? For some reason, I couldn't see it.

I poured us both a second cup of tea and passing the cup to Aunt Margaret, I said, "I can't see James Parfitt murdering Josephine Brown. The man I met wouldn't risk his baby son in such a way. Bunny said that himself, remember? I am in no doubt there is something iffy about him, but perhaps he's innocent?"

"Of spying, you mean?"

"Yes. Well, of all of it. They haven't any proof he's a mole, have they?"

"Not yet. But they don't usually place an undercover agent in a suspect's home without there being a very good reason."

"Well, we know it wasn't a robbery which rules out an opportunistic crime. But Nightingale was killed quickly and efficiently because of who she was, and what she either knew, or what they *thought* she knew. It was a professional job, Aunt Margaret. Perhaps it was this third party that Bunny spoke of?"

"And who do you suppose that could be? The Russians?"

"It's possible, isn't it?"

"Yes, but that would mean she was therefore on the right track and James Parfitt is an agent."

"Perhaps, but we don't know what she found out. It could be something else entirely. Something which points the finger at someone else. We're focusing on finding whoever killed Josephine Brown, correct? Well, just to play Devil's advocate, supposing it wasn't James Parfitt who killed her? But if not him then who? Oh dear, I feel as though I'm going around in circles."

I picked up my cup just as the clock in the lounge struck the hour. I stopped, teacup halfway to my lips as the elusive piece of information I'd been trying to grasp for days suddenly revealed itself.

"Ella, what is it?"

"It's the timing. I should have seen it earlier. It means James Parfitt was involved after all."

Chapter Eight

EARLY ON SATURDAY MORNING Aunt Margaret telephoned Bunny on his private line and arranged for us to meet. She explained I'd remembered some crucial information which placed, without doubt, James Parfitt in the middle of the murder investigation. Bunny suggested we contact Baxter immediately and then convene at the London Library in St. James's Square. It was a central meeting point for all of us and an unlikely place for us to be overheard. We were also to stagger our arrival times, so it wasn't obvious in the improbable event we were being watched, that we were meeting.

Aunt Margaret and I decided to take a taxi to the shopping district not far from our rendezvous point and do some shopping first. We felt it would be far less conspicuous to find ourselves outside the library on our return from a shopping trip and make an impromptu decision to go in than heading straight there.

So it was at ten past two that afternoon, laden with an impressive assortment of retail bags, we entered the London Library and made our way to the central stacks.

Immediately we recognised Carstairs at the far end. He sauntered towards us without any form of acknowledgment, but palmed a note to my aunt on his way past. It was all ludicrously cloak and dagger to me, especially considering we were the only ones there, but I assumed the intelligence service had survived for the last twenty-seven years because they knew what they were doing, so went along with it.

The note simply said **Committee Room**.

"What do you do now?" I whispered. "Tear it up into tiny pieces and eat the evidence?"

My aunt chuckled. "Of course. Unless you want to do the honours, dear? I find a dash of salt helps."

Both Baxter and Bunny were waiting for us when we entered. Bunny locked the door, and I saw Carstairs posted outside to ensure we weren't interrupted. Though heaven knows what we would do if we were. The room consisted of a long conference table, floor to ceiling glass-fronted bookshelves and an empty fireplace. The only possible hiding place was up the chimney. I was still working out how we'd all get up there when Bunny spoke.

"I don't have much time, Miss Bridges. What have you got to tell us?"

"On Tuesday afternoon, the day Miss Brown's body was found, Baxter and I went to interview the Parfitts. James Parfitt was still at work so we began by questioning Elizabeth alone. She told us that Miss Brown took the baby out at two o'clock every day and returned no earlier than four, just in time for tea. This was her routine six days a week and never changed."

"With you so far. How does that help us?"

I glanced at Baxter who was frowning. I suspect he was coming to the same realisation I had.

"Baxter, what time did James Parfitt report the nanny and Rupert missing?"

Baxter paged back through his notebook. "He stopped the constable at half-past three that afternoon, just as you were getting home with the bairn," he said slowly as he realised the import. "I can't believe I missed it," he said to me.

"I did too, Baxter. What were Parfitt's actual words, do you know?"

"Yes, the constable made a comprehensive report at the time. He said, 'My son is missing. I can't find my son.' The constable then asked who was with his son and Parfitt replied, 'His nanny.' 'So is the nanny missing as well, sir?' the constable asked, to which Parfitt replied, 'Yes.'"

"So his first words were that his son was missing, wholly understandable, but he didn't mention Miss Brown until prompted to do so, which to my mind, indicates prior knowledge of something having happened to her. I, of course, had taken the child home at that point, so to all intents and purposes, if James Parfitt knew where to look, and did so, then he would automatically assume his son was missing. Do you see?" I said, looking from Baxter to Bunny.

"Yes, I do," Baxter said, disgusted with himself. "Parfitt raised the alarm and reported his son missing half an hour before they would have been due home. He shouldn't have known the nanny and the boy were missing then if they usually got home at four."

"We know Parfitt probably wasn't responsible for Miss Brown's death," Bunny said, and at that moment I admired the man tremendously. Knowing what I knew about their real relationship he was holding things together remarkably well.

"Yes, I agree," I said. "You said yesterday, he wouldn't have left his son at risk if that was the case. But it certainly looks as though he knew who did it, arranged it himself even? Then he was contacted to say it had been done and where to find his son. When he couldn't find Rupert where he was told he'd been left, he panicked and got the police involved. If all had gone according to plan, we would never have known. James Parfitt collects his son and takes him home, making some excuse to his wife about how he found him alone or more likely that he'd arranged with Miss Brown to meet her and spend time with his son, giving her some time off. And we would have been none the wiser about Nightingale until she was found the next morning. But we wouldn't automatically have put two and two together."

"We would still have interviewed him though once we'd found out who she was. She was their nanny," Baxter said.

"But we wouldn't have found out who she was, Baxter. Without connecting the baby with the nanny and asking James Parfitt to come in and identify her, we would never have known. Parfitt could easily have said she was unreliable sometimes, meeting a lover perhaps or a friend. He may have formally lodged a fabricated missing person report, but it's most likely she would have been thought to have run off. He could easily have slanted the truth in any direction he wanted. He's a supposed foreign agent, the ability to lie convincingly is part of the job."

"But what about Mrs Parfitt?" Baxter asked.

"Elizabeth idolises her husband," I said. "To the extent that she would believe anything he told her. If he'd said he'd had to dismiss Miss Brown because she became unprofessional, for instance, Elizabeth would have believed him."

"Unprofessional in what way?"

"Well, perhaps he accused her of making a play for him behind Elizabeth's back, then when he refused, she became hysterical or threatening. That's not the sort of person you want as part of your household, let alone looking after your child. I'm not saying this is what he would have said, we'll never know how it would have played out now, but it's very easy to see how he could have got away with it."

"One thing is for sure though," Bunny said. "With Nightingale gone he either thinks he's safe or is running scared and wants out. I'm leaning toward the latter. This is where he'll make a mistake and when he does, we'll get him. I've also made the decision to keep Miss Brown's death quiet for now. Morale is low, what with us working on this case for so long and not finding the proof we need. I don't want to make it any worse. Especially as I'll need everyone on top form to deal with what's coming. This is the closest we've got to finding something on Parfitt and I'll not lose him now. If he thinks we aren't looking in his direction, he'll think he's got away with it. That's when he'll become careless."

We all agreed keeping the agent's murder under wraps was probably the wisest decision. However, with the power of hindsight it would prove to be a mistake.

"So, we need to have some sort of plan in place. Any suggestions?" Aunt Margaret asked Bunny.

"We already have an agent following him, but so far nothing. However, that was before all this came to light. Thanks to Baxter and Miss Bridges here, I'll double the guard and hope he shows his true colours. But what we really need is someone closer. Someone in his office for example."

"Well, Baxter and I are both out as he knows us."

There was a hush in the room as all heads swung to face my aunt. She rolled her eyes and looked at Bunny.

"Fancy coming out of retirement properly, Snow White?" he said with a grin.

———◆———

AUNT MARGARET AND I decided to walk back to Brunswick Gardens. We left ten minutes before the men, ensured we weren't being followed, then set off in the direction of Kensington Palace. It was a twenty-minute leisurely stroll and with the weather being overcast but dry and not particularly cold, it was quite pleasurable. It also gave us a chance to talk.

"Do you know, I find it utterly ironic that Gerry writes fictional spy thrillers, yet we're actually living the real life. A double life in actuality. If you include John, then all of us, except for mother and Ginny, are connected in some way or other to espionage."

"Oh yes, we're a regular family of spies, Ella. And don't forget what happened in the Riviera this summer. Elspeth is also loosely connected."

I'd temporarily forgotten about my mother's links to the intelligence community.

"Of course. Quite extraordinary, isn't it? And here you are, back out of retirement and about to infiltrate the Foreign Office as a secretary."

"Indeed. I'll have to brush up on my skills. My typing is fine but my Pitman shorthand is a little rusty."

"I truly doubt that, but if it is the case, then you only have a day and half to get up to speed. You start work on Monday morning, remember, assuming Bunny can make the arrangements that quickly."

"He will, Ella. Take my word for it. I know Bunny of old and I suspect this plan was put in place a while ago as an alternative option should the nanny position not work out. It will be a case of a simple telephone call or two and we'll be up and running with no one the wiser."

"Well, I shall help you practice when we get home if you'd like? By the way, how are we going to keep your absences from Gerry and Ginny?"

"Simple. I'm house hunting, darling. It's partly my reason for coming to London in the first place. And I think at some point I may take rooms at Claridges or perhaps rent a town house. It will give me a better opportunity to work incognito. Just to be on the safe side. You should come with me, darling. We'll be in contact then should we need to liaise in secret."

"I think that might be wise, Aunt Margaret. If things go according to plan it might very well become dangerous and I'd hate to put Gerry and Ginny at risk."

She linked her arm through mine. "It's better to err on the side of caution, dear. Incidentally, Baxter was rather furious with himself for missing the timing, wasn't he?"

"Yes, along with not realising that if I hadn't found the baby, then we'd have been unable to link the body with the Parfitts in the first place. Which is another clue to him not being himself. He wouldn't have missed those crucial points on any other occasion. I do wish I could help. I wonder what ails him?"

"Have you asked?"

"Not yet, I haven't really found an opportune moment to discuss it. But I will. I can't abide the idea he is suffering."

THE REMAINDER OF SATURDAY and the whole of Sunday passed quietly. We ate our meals with Gerry and Ginny, gently sowing seeds for Aunt Margaret's search for a London home and the fact she'd be absent more often than not.

When we were alone, I read aloud from *The Thirty-Nine Steps* and Aunt Margaret dutifully took it down in shorthand like a proper secretary, much to my amusement. As I surmised, it all came flooding back the moment she put pen to paper.

On Monday morning she left for the Foreign Office in a taxi and I was once again left to my own devices. We had a pre-arranged code should something happen, but for the first four days nothing did. Aunt Margaret returned from her day job each evening quite exhausted, but gamely made conversation at dinner with regard to the houses she'd viewed and how nothing was quite suitable. If I hadn't known any better, I would have believed every word.

By lunchtime on Friday, I was beginning to feel the odd combination of bored and slightly on edge. Foolishly, I had expected something to happen immediately Aunt Margaret had started work. In reality these sorts of things take time as I well knew. We were reliant on someone else making the first move, in this case James Parfitt, before we could jump into action. My problem was I had nothing to do and was feeling more than a little frustrated.

I think my feelings stemmed from the fact I felt both Baxter and I had been elbowed out of the case. While it had been ours to begin with, it had now turned into something much bigger, with more people involved and with potentially far-reaching consequences. I had no experience with espionage. Secret notes, codes and ciphers and the intelligence service was completely alien to me, and I didn't like the feeling of inadequacy. I was used to being pro-active and getting things done and I found myself chaffing at the necessity of having to pass certain tasks, ones which due to lack of experience and knowledge I could not do, onto someone else.

However, by the end of the week I had given myself a thorough talking to and was feeling much better. I wasn't usually one for self pity but I recognised this was exactly what I was doing. I was feeling sorry for myself and being a fool and quite selfish to boot. The only thing that mattered was to solve the case of Miss Brown's murder and assist in whatever way I could to catch a possible spy. Who performed the tasks necessary to achieve both, didn't matter.

At a quarter to four on Friday afternoon I'd almost resigned myself to another week of idleness when Betty came and informed me my aunt was on the telephone.

"Hello, darling, it's your aunt. I wondered if you'd like to meet me for tea today?"

This was it, the code phrase. Something was about to happen at last!

"Hello, Aunt. Yes, I'd love to. Shall I meet you at our usual place?"

"Yes, alright, dear, that would be perfect. Shall we say half-past five?"

"Lovely. I'll see you then."

"Oh, and bring an umbrella. It looks like rain."

The umbrella decree was new, but it must mean something, so I agreed then ended the call. It was time to catch a spy.

I IMMEDIATELY PICKED up the telephone again and made two calls. The first to Bunny and the second to Baxter informing them, in the words of one of my favourite literary characters, that 'The Game was Afoot'.

At five thirty on the dot I was standing beneath the Cenotaph War memorial in Whitehall, our pre-arranged meeting place, when I saw my aunt waving from the corner of the intersection between King Charles Street and Parliament Street. We began to walk towards each other just as I spied James Parfitt not a dozen yards behind her. I quickly put up the umbrella to shield my face just as my aunt reached me.

"You worked out what the umbrella was for then, dear? You always were my cleverest niece."

"Very amusing, Aunt Margaret." I was her only niece.

"I take it he's behind me?"

"Yes, shall we follow?"

"No need. Bunny's men will shadow him. I've already noticed Carstairs on foot and there's another two in a motor car in case he hails a taxi. But I know where he's going, so we can get there ahead of him. Come along, let's cross over before he sees us."

We hailed a vacant taxi outside The Red Lion, a Westminster public house with elaborate ceilings, portraits of well-known politicians and an illustrious clientele, according to my aunt.

"Brompton Oratory please, my good man. And there's an extra crown in it for you if you get us there quickly."

"Late for a service, Madam?"

"Oh no, dear. I suddenly have the urge to confess," she said in a slightly menacing way with a mad gleam in her eye.

I covered my face with my hand and swallowed down the desire to laugh. I felt the sudden surge of power as the car increased speed. Not I suspect due to the additional remuneration my aunt had promised, but more because he wanted her out of his vehicle as soon as possible.

But regardless of his reason we arrived within ten minutes, and with the extra money in his slightly shaking hand our taxi driver disappeared into the evening. No doubt with much relief and a tale to tell his wife, as we entered the church.

———◉———

BROMPTON ORATORY WAS a spectacular piece of neoclassical architecture. I knew of it of course, and had passed by several times when I'd found myself strolling around Knightsbridge or visiting the V&A, but had never had a reason to venture inside until now.

"How do you know he's coming here?" I asked Aunt Margaret as we entered the large double wooden doors.

"He telephoned a contact, and I happened to be within hearing distance."

"Gosh, isn't that a bit risky, calling from The Foreign Office?"

"Oh, we weren't in the office. It was lunchtime, and we were in the pub. Not together of course, I'd followed him. Don't worry, he didn't see me, but this place was mentioned and the time. To anyone else it would have sounded quite innocuous, but I recognised it for what it was."

"And what was that, a meeting?"

"No. I suspect it's a dead drop."

"You mean this is where he's passing over information? Will we meet his contact then?"

"Yes and no."

"You're taking this spy business far too much to heart, Aunt Margaret. No need to be quite so enigmatic. Please explain."

"Sorry, dear. Yes, this is where he passes the information but no, we will not see the contact. This is a dead drop, so called as the two parties don't meet. As opposed to a live drop where they do."

"Ah, I see. Thank you."

"You're welcome. Now, he'll be here shortly and we need to be seated somewhere inconspicuous."

"Where we can see him but he can't see us," I said.

"Precisely."

"Well, that shouldn't be too difficult. Just pick a pillar," I said in whispered awe as we entered the church proper.

The interior was an absolute wonder. A successful hybrid of mainly Italian Renaissance with some Roman Baroque styling. Pilasters and columns were made from Devon Marble. I remembered a holiday we'd had as children in Torquay one year, where the marble works were based, and recognised its distinctive array of colours, textures and fossils.

There were more exotic marbles used in the apse and the altars, with carvings in metalwork, plasterwork, wood and stone. Several statues stood on plinths, including The Twelve Apostles. The ceiling was domed with a cupola, and reflecting the rest of the church, highly decorative. It really was absolutely breathtaking.

"Did you know Alfred Hitchcock was married here in '26?" my aunt whispered as we reached the halfway mark.

"No, I didn't. Were you invited?"

She gave me a knowing smile but said nothing. "Elgar too in 1889."

"Were you invited to that one as well?"

"How old do you think I am, dear?"

"Ageless and timeless, Aunt Margaret."

"Oooo, very good answer, Ella. Now, I think we'll split up at this juncture. You take this side, I'll go across the aisle. If you see anything don't move, just observe. Surreptitiously."

"Yes, alright." I lowered the veil on my hat, obscuring my face and took a seat behind a column wreathed in shadow, which would shield me from anyone coming in, but would give me a clear line of sight to both the entrance door and the far end of the church. Across the other side, a bit further down, Aunt Margaret did the same.

Then we waited.

Chapter Nine

APART FROM THE THUDDING of my own heart, the inside of the Oratory was completely silent. My aunt and I were the only two inside, and I wondered if Bunny's men had somehow kept away any other worshippers.

Approximately five minutes after I'd sat down there was a faint click as the main door opened, then a soft thud as it closed again. The sound of a muffled footfall on the elaborately inlaid wooden floor increased in volume as it got closer, and I lowered my head as if in prayer, all the while watching from beneath my brow for the person to whom they belonged.

Suddenly he came into view. It was James Parfitt.

I observed him go to the front, genuflect before the altar and remain there for a moment, head bowed as if in prayer. Suddenly I felt my bile rise. What on earth was he doing? Here was a man who was passing our government's secrets to an enemy power. Was he praying for forgiveness? Expecting to be absolved of all his sins? I was filled with contempt for his hypocrisy and it took all of my willpower to remain in place and not confront him. I clenched my fists in my lap and took a deep breath to calm myself as I continued to watch him. He rose, made the sign of the cross and walked to the front wall where he slipped something between the pillars, then turned and left the way he had come, unhurried and seemingly without a care in the world. Had it all been an act? I truly couldn't say. It was all so seamless and innocent-looking and had I not known what he was really doing I wouldn't have been suspicious in the slightest.

I remained where I was even after Parfitt had left. I knew Bunny's men would have picked him up immediately, quickly and quietly. What we needed now was the person who was due to retrieve whatever he'd hidden.

Two of Bunny's men joined us not long after James Parfitt had left and we sat there for a further twenty minutes. Eventually, my aunt rose and beckoned me to follow. The SIS men ignored us, staying in place.

Outside my aunt and I walked in the direction of Kensington Park in silence lest we were being followed, but when I deemed we were alone I asked what would happen next?

"Bunny's men will stay there for a while yet to see if anyone comes to collect Parfitt's communication. Although I doubt they will. It would have happened by now otherwise. I'm sorry to say, but I think we've been rumbled."

"Well, at least we caught Parfitt in the act."

"Indeed. I also think the other side know we have him, unfortunately."

"Where will they take him?"

"To one of the many undisclosed locations the Secret Intelligence Service keeps for such a contingency. Sometimes it's best not to know, Ella."

"Will you still need to go to work on Monday? I know you're Parfitt's personal secretary, albeit a temporary one, but he won't be there, will he?"

"No, he won't but as a simple secretary I wouldn't know that. I'll speak to Bunny and see what he thinks is best. Now, how about some dinner?"

"We're hardly dressed for dinner, Aunt Margaret."

"Don't worry, I know a little place where dressing is optional."

I didn't reply. Unsurprisingly, I couldn't think of a suitable rejoinder.

MY AUNT'S IDEA OF 'a little place' was a three-storey private members' club in Soho named The Gargoyle. It occupied the upper floors of a pair of elegant Georgian town houses, the ground floor being home to a printing works. I had expected to enter through a door but she led me around the corner from Dean Street to Meard Street. After flashing her membership credentials, we stepped into a rickety external lift, enclosed in shining metal like an old-fashioned steamer trunk, with two other people I vaguely recognised but couldn't put a name to, and began our ascent.

"We'll go all the way to the top to start with, darling. I think you'll like it up there."

"To the roof?"

I couldn't possibly see what interest a roof would have for me, but I bowed to my aunt's obvious knowledge of the place and waited. Imagine my surprise when we stepped out into a perfectly wonderful garden. It was set up for dining and dancing and all around, the chimneys of the neighbouring buildings were painted a bright vibrant red. I'd never seen anything like it.

"Oh, it's marvellous! What a perfectly wonderful idea to put a garden on a roof."

"Wait until you see the rest of the place."

"I don't think it can get any better than this, Aunt Margaret."

But of course I was wrong. The whole place was a lavish mix of high society and Bohemia. A theatrical social setting where the upper crust rubbed shoulders with those in the arts.

We went downstairs to the bar, a bright and tastefully decorated area with several paintings by Matisse adorning the walls, whom my aunt informed me was a member and responsible for much of the interior decor. It was a vivacious spot, crowded with people discussing art and politics, and Aunt Margaret ordered a Pimms with a dash of Curacao, a house specialty and delicious.

From there I was given the tour of the other rooms. A very large ballroom with, of all things, a fountain in the dance floor. The Tudor room, a coffee room and a drawing room. Then we moved to the restaurant via a stunning staircase in glittering steel and brass. Again, designed by Matisse. The room had been modelled on the Alhambra at Granada with an elaborate coffered ceiling painted with gold leaf. The walls were adorned with imperfectly cut-glass tiles which reflected the light and clientele beautifully, and the whole thing was topped off by a wonderful four-piece band delivering lively, cheerful music.

We were led to a table for two on the outer edge of the room and in the spirit of the place, my aunt ordered a bottle of the finest Club 'fizz.'

"I'm really quite astonished, Aunt Margaret," I said as our Oysters arrived. "As soon as I think I know everything there is to know about you, you do something like this and completely knock my socks off."

She laughed. "I thought you'd appreciate it, Ella."

"Oh, I really do. I adore the place, it's the perfect antidote to murder and espionage and just what I needed. How long have you been a member?"

"Since the beginning. I was here for opening night, let's see, nearly twelve years ago. Gosh, that's flown by. I don't come often, of course, but it's lovely to experience it all again through your eyes."

We finished our course of French Onion soup topped with crispy croutons, then over the main course of Duck our conversation inevitably turned to the case.

"So, really the case is almost over, what with you-know-who being caught earlier?" I didn't want to mention any names in case we were overheard, but actually I realised it would be unlikely. No one was taking any notice of us, and what with the general level of noise combined with the band I doubt they could eavesdrop successfully.

"I'm afraid not, Ella. It's just the beginning. Parfitt wasn't working alone."

"Did Bunny tell you that?"

"He did, during our private tête-à-tête."

"So what happens next?"

"Parfitt will be interrogated and..."

"Questioned, you mean?"

"Not quite."

"What's the difference?" I asked, although I wasn't sure I wanted to know.

"One is a little more... intense than the other, shall we say?"

I looked down and frowned, taking a moment to fill my fork. Did I really want to be a party to this?

"I know it's difficult to comprehend, Ella. And I don't always agree with the methods used by the intelligence services, but I'm afraid it happens, and not just here. The fact is the security of our country is at stake and we need that information. I know it sounds melodramatic, but it's the truth."

I nodded. "Go on."

"Parfitt will be interrogated and hopefully give up his sources and his contacts. As well as his colleagues, those who are working as agents for the Russians. Then we try to turn him back."

"A triple agent?"

"Yes. Complicated, isn't it? But Bunny has managed it before. After that we put a plan in motion that will provide the proof we need to catch the others in his spy ring, and his Russian counterpart if possible."

"What if he doesn't confess?"

"I think we have to assume he will for the moment, Ella. It will get very nasty very quickly otherwise. The man has a lot to lose if he doesn't comply. Not least his wife and child."

"I see. But I'm not sure what more I can do. My initial case is over." I was beginning to feel frustrated and left out again. I was disappointed in myself but couldn't seem to help it.

"I know, dear. But I expect I'll still need to be involved. In fact, I think Bunny will insist upon it. I could do with a partner, someone I trust implicitly to watch my back and there's no one I would rather have than you."

Really, when she put it like that how could I refuse?

CARSTAIRS TELEPHONED Aunt Margaret on Saturday morning to inform us no one had turned up for the package Parfitt had left and she wouldn't be needed back at work. My aunt had been right in assuming we'd been rumbled. He also informed her that Bunny would be in touch via their old method soon.

Subsequently, for the following three days my aunt insisted on us visiting an area of Broadway, where she asked for a box of England's Glory matches from a blind match seller. For three days he apologised and said he had none, but assured her he'd have some the next day.

I was beginning to wonder if he'd ever have any when on the fourth day he finally handed her a box, took remuneration far exceeding the face price of the goods, and wished her a good afternoon.

She put the box in her bag and made no mention of it until we returned home for tea. For the next few days, we would be alone except for the staff, as Gerry and Ginny were staying with her parents. Rather fortuitous as it happened.

"Let's see what Bunny has to say, shall we?" She opened the matchbox and unfurled a piece of thick paper. "He's sending a car for us tonight at ten o'clock. He needs our help apparently."

"With Parfitt?"

"I assume so. We'll find out when we get there."

"And where exactly is *there*, Aunt Margaret?"

"I couldn't say. It will be one of those secret places I mentioned to you before."

"Why so late?"

"The Secret Intelligence Service don't keep normal office hours, especially when questioning a suspect. Now, I suggest we have a rest after tea. We should try to get some sleep. We could have a long night ahead of us. Of course, if you'd rather stay here, I'll understand?"

"No, it's alright I'll come along. I may be of use, you never know."

I tried very hard not to sound petulant, but the raising of an eyebrow told me I hadn't succeeded as well as I'd thought. Thankfully she didn't pursue the matter and shortly after we went to rest.

———— ◉ ————

AT TEN O'CLOCK THAT evening there was a knock at the door and my aunt and I went to answer it. We'd told Betty and the other staff to get an early night and informed them we'd be out until the early hours with friends.

The man that had knocked stood by the open door of the shiny black Ford motor car parked at the kerb, and my aunt and I slipped into the back. He lowered the passenger seat, seated himself, then the driver pulled away. Not a word was spoken the entire time.

We headed out of the city in a southerly direction, and not far beyond the city limits, the driver pulled over and the man in the passenger seat turned and handed us a black strip of cloth each.

"Please, put them on."

"A blindfold? Whatever for?" my aunt said.

"Orders, Madam," he said and then faced forward.

It was obvious they had no intention of continuing the journey until we'd complied. Aunt Margaret gave me a quick glance which sent a frisson of fear down my spine, then tied the cloth around her eyes. I sighed. In for a penny in for a pound I thought, and did the same. Once again the car began to move.

We'd only been travelling for approximately ten minutes when I had a paralysing thought. We didn't know who these men were! We'd just assumed they'd been sent by Bunny as per the note in the matchbox but we'd had no additional code to use and considering the agency's penchant for the theatrical this was worrying in the extreme. In fact, no words had been spoken at all apart from the demand to wear the eye covering, and I didn't recognise either one of them as being in Bunny's company previously. We'd just blithely entered the vehicle without a second thought and we'd questioned nothing. We were quite literally blind and in a motor car with two complete strangers!

What if the match seller had switched the message? Perhaps the 'other side' had given him more money? God knows he looked as though he needed it. We could be in the car with two Russian spies and being taken to a secluded place to be done away with. They'd never find our bodies!

I began to breathe heavily, my heart pounding in my chest as the fear began to take hold. There was no way out of this vehicle, we were trapped in the back! Suddenly I felt Aunt Margaret's hand grasp my own and squeeze tightly. Either she'd reached the same conclusion I had or she was trying to reassure me. I truly didn't know and it would be a mistake to voice my concerns so I remained silent, but squeezed her hand in reply.

All we could do now was wait and see where we ended up and pray it wouldn't be in a ditch.

Chapter Ten

ALL IN ALL, THE JOURNEY took just under three quarters of an hour. We'd driven along flat roads, up steep hills and slight inclines. Around corners both left and right and along quiet deserted roads. I had absolutely no idea which direction we'd taken but eventually we stopped and I heard the opening of a gate, we presumably continued through and came to a stop at the end of a bumpy track.

"You can remove your blindfolds now," the front passenger said, and I heard the motor car door open.

Relieved, I took off the cloth binding my eyes and threw it on the back parcel shelf, catching Aunt Margaret's eye as I did so.

"Don't worry, Ella, we'll be fine."

We exited the car just as Bunny came striding across the yard. I had never been so relieved to see anyone in my life and slumped against the motor, willing my knees not to give way.

"Snow White, Miss Bridges, thank you for coming."

"Bunny, a word," my aunt said with barely concealed fury.

It was obvious to all present that Bunny was about to get a severe dressing down. The two men who'd brought us shared a look, and a raised eyebrow or two, then made themselves scarce. I wished I could do the same, but I had no idea where I was. It looked like an abandoned farmhouse with various out-buildings, currently deep in shadow, but I knew looks could be deceiving and I didn't want to inadvertently wander somewhere I wasn't supposed to be, like a practice shooting ground, so I stayed put.

My aunt and Bunny had disappeared around the corner of the main building out of sight, but I could still hear the odd word drifting toward me on the still night's air. Words such as threatened, terrified and imbecile. Eventually the fiery onslaught ceased, and the words were lost in the reduced volume, replaced with contrite mumbling. Bunny apologising, I assumed. A few minutes later they both reappeared and my aunt gave me a brief smile and a wink. We followed Bunny to a small outbuilding where we descended the steps underneath a concealed trapdoor into what I assumed was a bunker. Didn't anyone in the Secret Intelligence Service work above ground?

We walked down a short corridor, then Bunny showed us into a plain office with only the bare essentials.

"I think I owe you an apology, Miss Bridges. We should have put an additional code in place so you knew who was picking you up. An oversight and entirely my fault. It won't happen again."

As he was talking he'd produced a bottle of brandy and three glasses from the filing cabinet on the back wall. I took the proffered drink with a slight shake in my hand and knocked it back in one, relishing the warmth as it suffused my chest and steadied my tingling nerves.

"Thank you," I said, replacing the glass on the desk. I was pleased to note my hand was once again steady.

"Another? he asked, bottle poised.

"No. One was sufficient, thank you."

"You can refill mine," my aunt said. "Now, why are we here, Bunny? I assume you're having problems with Parfitt?"

"Yes. He's stronger than he looks. Quite frankly he's given us sod all so far. Even presented with the evidence of the dead drop he's professing his innocence. Says he was coerced under threat of losing his life. Complete rubbish of course. We've also presented him with various names of his colleagues, hoping to find the rest of his ring, but he's denying he knows anything. He's lying. But I can't work out when. I'm hoping you can help."

"You've tried to break him, I suppose?"

He gave me a quick glance, then nodded. "The usual methods, but he's given us nothing. Think you can get us something?"

"Probably, although I'd say Ella is even better. She wrote *The Art of the Lie* for Scotland Yard, you know. They use it extensively as part of the approved method for interviewing criminals."

"Did she now? Well, I'm very glad you're here in that case, Miss Bridges."

"What have you told Elizabeth Parfitt about her husband's absence?" I asked.

"We've telephoned from The Foreign Office and informed her he's away on important Government business. We'll send a letter reportedly from him in a day or two just to reinforce the message. She's perfectly accepting of what she's been told and will be none the wiser for the time being."

"Alright, Bunny. I suppose we had better get on with it then," Aunt Margaret said. "Lead the way."

IT WAS WITH SOME TREPIDATION I followed Bunny and my aunt to the room next to where James Parfitt was being held. I didn't know exactly what 'the usual methods' entailed, but I could make an educated guess and I didn't like it one bit. I was dreading seeing him in person.

The room we were in was small and narrow with a viewing window through which we could see inside the interrogation room. A long bench with high stools provided a place for us to sit and work, while watching the proceedings in the main room.

James Parfitt was seated at a table bolted to the floor. His clothes were crumpled, and he looked as though he hadn't slept since the night he'd been captured. His lip was split and one eye was blackened. He looked simply dreadful. Sallow complexion, hollow cheeks and haunted eyes. But there was a fire in them too. He wasn't going to go down without a fight.

I hardened my heart against the depravity and reminded myself that here was a man that had not only put his baby son at risk, but was complicit in the murder of his nanny. He was also a traitor.

"Can he see us?" I asked Bunny.

"No. It's a two-way mirror. All he can see is the reflection of the room he's in. He can't hear us either."

I looked at a speaker on the wall next to the bench. "What's this for?"

"So you can hear what's being said inside. There's a switch next to it. Turn it on when you're ready."

He sighed and leant against the back wall, folding his arms.

"Look, I know you both have been thrust into this, if not unwillingly then at least accidentally, and I want you to know your help is much appreciated."

"I feel a 'but' coming on, Bunny," Aunt Margaret said.

"Yes, and it's a big one. If we don't get something from Parfitt soon the whole game could be up. The dead drop was a bust as you know. No one came for what he'd left which means they know we've got him. Whoever he's working with will be scrambling now to wrap things up and get out. We need the identity of these men urgently before we lose them completely."

"What's happened to the documents Parfitt left at the Church?" I asked.

"We've got them. I've got a team of professional code-breakers going through it all, but so far nothing. Parfitt is our only hope at this juncture. I need you to help me get those names. Now. Tonight."

"We'll obviously do our best," I said. "We know what to look for, but it will all depend on how well trained he is. However, I also want you to find out what he knows about Miss Brown's death. We know he's involved somehow. Even if he didn't dirty his own hands he knows who did."

"I fully intend to, Miss Bridges."

"Bunny," my aunt said, "I would also suggest at some point you mention his wife and child. Not until we've hopefully got what we need regarding his fellow spies, but perhaps toward the end? From what Ella has told me he loves his wife, but his son means everything to him."

"That's right," I said. "If he thinks they are going to be in some sort of danger, then he's more likely to cooperate. I find it a distasteful thing to do but as you say we need answers quickly. But you must promise me nothing untoward will happen to Elizabeth or Rupert Parfitt? They are innocent. I would like your word, Bunny, your solemn oath before we do anything else. Do I have it?"

"Yes, Miss Bridges, you do. Elizabeth Parfitt will know nothing until the time comes when we have to tell her her husband is accused of treason. And even then, we will continue to do all we can to help her move forward. So, going back to the plan, the threat of arresting his wife as being an accomplice should unhinge him enough to start talking, yes? Actually, that's more than feasible. Surely you can't live with someone for so long and not pick up on some of what they're doing? Unless you're Mrs Parfitt of course. Now, you're positive she doesn't know anything?"

"Yes, I am. She's an adoring wife and mother with a professional husband. Hers is an old-fashioned attitude, I'm afraid, which is why she hasn't picked up any clues as to his true motives. He goes to work and provides for the family and she runs the household and brings up the children. She would never ask her husband about his work, she'd wait until he volunteered the information. Even then I doubt she'd understand what he was telling her."

"Alright. So, we'll tell him his wife is suspected of collaborating with him, and that left with no choice we'll have to remove the child into the care of an orphanage or the church? Yes, that would do it."

"But not until after we've had a chance to get what you need, the other names."

"Why?"

"Because in a state of high agitation, which he'll be in if he thinks his child and wife are at risk, he'll tell you whatever he thinks you want to know. Even if it's a pack of lies."

"I thought that was your area of expertise?"

I nodded. "It is, but it needs to be in a controlled situation. The small 'tells' which will allow me to read him and prove he's lying won't be discernible if he's panicking and emotional. He needs to think he's dominating the conversation and manipulating you, and, to some extent, that you believe him. Pandering to his ego if you will. It's a difficult balance to get right, but I daresay you've had plenty of experience."

"Sadly, that's true, Miss Bridges. It's part of my job, unsavoury as it is."

"Well, I suggest you use the ploy against his family toward the end to see what he can tell us about Josephine Brown's murder."

"Alright, I'll bow to your proficiency in this area, Miss Bridges, and do as you say. Now, if you're both ready, let's see what we can find out."

"Just one more thing," I said. "Is Parfitt left or right-handed?"

"Right. Is that important?"

"Yes. I need to know his dominant side otherwise I can't tell when a reaction is false."

———◉———

AFTER BUNNY HAD LEFT the room to find the colleague who would be accompanying him, my aunt asked me how I was bearing up?

"Not too well, I'm afraid. I don't understand this world, Aunt Margaret. I consult and investigate crimes where the motives are more simple. Jealousy, love, hatred, money. Treason I can't comprehend at all. James Parfitt is British, he's a Cambridge man working for our Government. Well off financially and with a loving family. What makes a man turn his back on all that and willfully destruct the very essence of what it means to be British? And for the Russians of all people? What on earth does he have in common with Russia that he would be willing to betray his own country for? What happened to his patriotism? To his loyalty?"

Aunt Margaret shook her head. "I don't know, Ella, I truly don't. And it's a pointless exercise trying to fathom what's going on in his mind. We are not, nor will we ever be, privy to his internal thoughts, to what experiences he has had that have led him ultimately to betray his country and to find himself here. The only one who can answer those questions is sitting in the next room."

"And that's another thing," I continued. "They're using techniques here that are quite simply torture. He's obviously not been allowed to sleep since he arrived. Has he been allowed food? Water? We can see he's been beaten. What next, the rack? Thumb-screws? It's as though we've been cast back into the dark ages. I'm not sure I can be a party to it."

"You won't need to be, Ella. This is simply questioning him so you and I can determine if he's lying. There will be nothing brutish, I promise, although Bunny will undoubtedly raise his voice. You've seen for yourself it's one of his shortcomings. But that's it, no more physical torment. That part is over. It didn't work. If we can get what we need tonight, then that will be the end of it. Bunny may attempt to turn him back; it will depend on whether we get what we've come for, but if he doesn't succeed, then he'll be moved from here and probably sent to prison where he'll await trial."

She stood up and wrapped her arms around me. "I'm so sorry, darling, I shouldn't have brought you here. I should have dealt with it myself. You need a hard heart in this line of work and yours is still young and full of love, and to a certain extent idealism."

I stiffened slightly.

"It's far from being an insult, Ella. You really have no idea how proud I am of you. I don't want you to lose your innocence, it's what makes you who you are. But the world, I'm sorry to say, isn't filled with just good and bad people or choices that are simply right or wrong. It's rather murkier than that, I'm afraid. Sometimes good people have to do bad things but for the right reason. What's happening here is a case in point. This man Parfitt is not only putting the security of our country at risk but the lives of the agents we currently have abroad. If he passes on information which gives the code names and real identities of those agents, then they will lose their lives. Then their families will also suffer. It's all about the bigger picture, Ella."

She pulled me from her embrace and held me by my shoulders, looking into my eyes for the truth before she asked the question.

"Do you want to leave, because I will understand if you do?"

I shook my head. "No. I'll be alright. It's helped to talk to you, Aunt Margaret, thank you. Besides, I have a job to do."

She smiled. "Of course it's helped. I do talk sense sometimes, you know. Well done, darling. Oh, it looks as though Bunny is ready. Do you want to switch on the speaker please, dear?"

I leaned across and flipped the switch, then retrieved my notebook and pen from my bag. We both settled at the bench and waited to see what we would learn.

"I do hope this works, Ella."

"Do you know, I think it might actually."

"Oh, why is that?"

"Because Phantom has just appeared."

⸺●⸺

AS THE INTERROGATION began, Carstairs joined us to watch the proceedings. Bunny and he had worked out another 'play' apparently, and he was waiting for his cue.

The questioning of Parfitt took another hour, with Bunny attempting to catch him out in lies several times. It was a well-known method; asking the same question myriad times in several contrasting ways, hoping for a different answer. James Parfitt was clever though and didn't slip up once.

Bunny raised his voice several times, slamming his fist on the table to reinforce his point, then took an about turn and became friendly and cajoling, but again this had no effect. Parfitt remained sometimes contrite and reasonable, but in the main arrogant and cock-sure, his face smirking several times as he continually protested his innocence and claimed to be the victim, in fear for his life at the time if he didn't do what he'd been told.

"How did you get these instructions? Who was it that gave them to you?" Bunny asked.

I watched closely as James Parfitt replied.

"A note at work. It was on my desk when I arrived. I have no idea who sent it."

That last statement was a lie. His eyes had darted back and forth. He was beginning to feel uncomfortable and trapped by the questions.

"And where is this note now?" Bunny continued.

"I destroyed it, like I was asked to. I've already told you all this. If you have nothing new to add then you can't keep me here."

"Actually, Mr Parfitt, I can. Now, I'd like to go through your friends and colleagues. We know you're part of a bigger circle and if you give me those names, then I may be able to be a bit more lenient with your punishment."

"But I've told you already! How many more times do I have to say it? I don't know what you are talking about. I was coerced just once and under threat of death!"

Parfitt's heightened emotion made ascertaining this lie a little more difficult, but the pursing of the lips and the sucking motion indicated this proclamation was also not the truth. A person's mouth tends to go dry when they are lying.

Bunny eyed him coldly, then began to recite the names of a number of Parfitt's work colleagues, his friends, those he socialised with in any form no matter how infrequently. Aunt Margaret and I watched closely and made notes.

All the time Phantom sat at the back wall and never took his eyes from Parfitt.

The first two names garnered very little response, but the third, Arnister, caused him to close his eyes for a second or two, as well as touch his face. Both indicators he was lying. People have a tendency to blink rapidly when not telling the truth, closing their eyes prevents this. Their faces also itch. There was no doubt Parfitt knew this person well and that he was most likely a part of the same spy ring. The fourth name, Batholomew, had the same effect. Parfitt was also beginning to sweat. I had at least two names that needed to be pursued. The rest of the list, like the first two, elicited no worthwhile responses.

Eventually, having seemingly got nowhere Bunny threw down his pen and leaned back, folding his arms.

"That's my cue," Carstairs said and left the room. A moment later he knocked on the interview room door. Bunny turned.

"What is it?"

"There's been a development, sir."

Bunny stood up and went to the door and Carstairs and he had a murmured discussion. But not too quietly for I distinctly heard Carstairs speak the word wife.

"What about the boy?" Bunny whispered none too quietly.

Carstairs whispered something about an orphanage and Bunny nodded.

All the while I was watching the face of James Parfitt, who had gone from being arrogant and assured to puzzled and then horrified as the reality of what he was hearing sunk in.

"Wait!" he cried out.

But Bunny ignored him and left the room with Carstairs, closing the door.

Seconds later both men were standing behind us.

"Right, we'll let him stew in there for a bit. Did you find what we were looking for?"

"Yes, I did," I said.

I handed my notes to Aunt Margaret with the two names I had underlined and she nodded.

"I concur," she said, showing me where she'd written down the same two names.

"So, who are we looking for?" Bunny asked.

"The first is Edward Bartholomew and the second Richard Arnister."

"Good God, those two, eh? Well done, Miss Bridges, Snow White. You've done sterling work here tonight."

"Who are they?" I asked.

"Bartholomew is a senior diplomatic correspondent with The News Chronicle, a daily run out of Fleet Street. Arnister is a Professor of Literature at the University of London. He's a member of the Athenaeum Club too. It's where Parfitt met him, I think. I'll have my men follow them immediately and see what we can find."

"They've been placed well, haven't they?" my aunt said.

"Oh, yes. Particularly Bartholomew, who travels extensively and has contacts in all the British Embassies abroad. But do you know what's more worrying? The fact they've been in these positions for years."

Chapter Eleven

IN THE EARLY HOURS of Thursday morning my aunt and I once again entered the motor car with the two gentlemen who'd picked us up and were returned home. This time however there were no blind-folds. Although it would have made little difference as minutes into the journey we were both fast asleep.

We were aroused by the jolt of the car coming to a halt outside the house and once through the door we staggered upstairs to our beds.

Before we'd left Bunny had informed us he would continue his questioning of James Parfitt. With his family now being under suspicion, a ruse he was unaware of, Bunny expected to get some informative answers. He would be in contact sometime in the days ahead to let us know both what he learned, and to discuss a plan to enable us to prove Bartholomew and Arnister were in fact double agents and, more importantly, a plan in which to catch them.

I had nodded politely when he told us but was too emotionally exhausted to take it all in. It was with no surprise therefore that, back in the safe and familiar surroundings of my room, as soon as my head hit the pillow I was out like a light.

Naturally we missed breakfast on Thursday morning, but met in the orangerie for brunch. It took one cup of tea and two cups of coffee before I felt human enough to speak. My aunt felt the same.

"When are our travellers due to return?"

"Late on Sunday afternoon, I believe," I replied. "Although knowing Gerry he'll insist on being back for tea. Why do you ask?"

"Because the case we're on is about to get more complicated and I suspect Bunny will call upon us for help. If that's the case, it's likely our working hours are going to be unconventional, to say the least. I think it's about time we moved, Ella. What say you?"

I smiled. "You're right as usual, Aunt Margaret. Where did you have in mind?"

"Claridges. It's central enough for all our needs."

"As well as being the height of luxury."

"Of course, darling. Did you expect otherwise? We might have a dirty job to do but there's no need to live in the same way. I'll telephone them this afternoon and make arrangements for Monday. I do hope Gerry and Ginny will understand."

"They will, don't worry. They know we lead slightly unconventional lives and that I have a current case to work on. Besides, it's only in Mayfair, so not too far away."

"Very true on all counts, dear. So, what do you want to do for the next few days?"

"Honestly? Absolutely nothing. I don't want to make plans at all, just rest and read and perhaps play cards, if you're willing? The odd walk around the Palace Gardens for fresh air will suit me just fine. Unless of course you wish to do something in particular?"

"Not at all. Your ideas sound perfectly wonderful. We are likely to have a busy time ahead of us so resting while we can makes very good sense. Just don't be too disappointed when you lose at cards, dear. I've hustled with the best of them in Monte Carlo, I'll have you know."

I laughed. "I'm not surprised in the least. Wasn't it Somerset Maugham who said it was a 'sunny place for shady people?'"

AUNT MARGARET AND I spent a pleasurable few days pleasing ourselves. Neither Bunny nor Baxter had telephoned, and we relished the peace and quiet and the companionship.

On Sunday at a quarter to three, Ginny and Gerry returned and after a brief rest we all met up for tea in the drawing room.

"Did you have a lovely break?" I asked.

"It was super," Ginny replied. "Very restful and lovely to see everyone again. Mummy has had my old nursery redecorated in shades of yellow and white and Daddy is already discussing the possibility of a pony. They are terribly excited about their first grandchild."

"Yes, I can see that. Quite right too. What about you, Gerry, did you get any work done?"

"Some. But the book's first iteration is complete, just editing to do now, so I took the opportunity for a break too."

"He spent quite a bit of time at the local watering hole with my Father."

"Had to be done, darling," Gerry said to his wife. "The locals expect to see the Lord of the Manor on occasion and your father was happy to oblige. It's good for morale."

"It's a chance for them to relieve you of your money playing billiards, you mean."

Gerry laughed. "See, I told you it was good for morale. So what about you two?" Gerry asked Aunt Margaret and I. "What's happening with the case?"

"It's moving along as a matter of fact. Aunt Margaret has been a terrific help."

"Do you know what happened to that poor nanny then?" Ginny said, handing me an egg and cress sandwich.

I nodded. "Yes, we think so. We're just trying to prove it."

"What about the house hunting, Aunt Margaret? Any luck?"

"Nothing quite suitable as yet, Gerry, dear. But I'm sure there'll be something along shortly. Which reminds me. Now, I don't want either of you to take this the wrong way, I adore staying with you both, you know that, but I have made arrangements to move into Claridges tomorrow and Ella has very graciously agreed to accompany me."

"My work is not subject to normal hours, you see, and Aunt Margaret will be house hunting and I suspect visiting friends. We really don't want to disturb either of you with our comings and goings. Of course, Claridges isn't too far away so we can visit regularly."

To mine and my aunt's amazement, Ginny and Gerry shared a look, then began to laugh.

"Oh, honestly, you two," Gerry said. "There's no need for all the excuses. Do you think we don't know what's really going on? Don't worry, your secrets are safe with us," he said, tapping the side of his nose.

"I have no idea what you're talking about," my aunt said with a smirk.

"Nor I," I chimed in.

"Of course you don't, darlings," Ginny said. "Just promise us one thing? That you'll stay safe and look after each other?"

———◉———

WITH OUR BAGS PACKED and already en route to Claridges, Aunt Margaret and I bid farewell to Ginny and Gerry with promises to see them soon.

My Aunt had reserved suite 212 for an extended period and once we had signed in and obtained our key from the concierge, we rode the Otis lift to our floor, sitting on the comfortable settee while the attendant operated the controls.

"Have you stayed here before, Ella, I can't remember?"

"There's never been a need to. With Ginny and Gerry so close, if I've come to the city I've always stayed with them."

"You are in for a treat in that case, darling. I adore this place and the suite is my very favourite."

We exited the lift close to our rooms and Aunt Margaret gave the attendant some coin and thanked him.

Opening the door, she led me into the entrance hall and through to the large living room, where an original Gilbert and Sullivan grand piano stood in pride of place by one of the three bay windows, with views onto Brook Street and Davies Street. There was a marble fireplace with delicately-carved details, on top of which stood an ormolu clock and a family of five small china pigs. An antique Louis XV style desk with gilded accents stood in the second bay and a round antique dining table, which seated four, in the third. Mouldings and features sat alongside Victorian-era garlanded acanthus plasterwork, all of which set a truly palatial scene.

There were two bedrooms both en-suite, and the master which my aunt took also had its own dressing room. Fresh flowers were in vases on several tables throughout the suite and gave off a delicate and fresh floral scent.

"I can certainly see why you adore it here, Aunt Margaret," I said, taking a seat on one of the exceptionally plush settees. "It must be like staying at Buckingham Palace."

"And you wouldn't be wrong, dear. It's almost an extension of the palace itself. Many of the crowned heads of Europe stay here. I suspect there's a few of them in residence now as a matter of fact, but of course one of the beauties of Claridges, apart from our personal Butler and its timeless English glamour of course, is its discretion. Perfect for our needs, wouldn't you say?"

"Unquestionably. And speaking of our needs, I'll just put a call through to The Yard and let Baxter know where we are."

"Excellent idea, Ella. I have a feeling that Bunny will contact us before long."

She was correct. He telephoned later that evening. And he had a plan.

⸻ ◉ ⸻

HAVING HAD A LIGHT lunch in the dining room and afternoon tea in the reading room, we organised dinner for three to be served in our suite. Bunny would be joining us at half-past eight and we would be dining at nine.

As the ormolu clock on the marble mantelpiece delicately chimed the half hour, there was a knock at the door and our butler showed Bunny in.

"Ladies," he said with a small bow. He was dressed in an impeccably tailored evening dress. I hardly recognised the uncouth SIS man I'd met previously.

"Hello, Bunny. Come in and sit down. Would you like a drink?"

"Please, Snow. A Scotch if you have one."

Aunt Margaret poured a healthy glass of Johnny Walker Swing and handed it to him, leaving the distinctively shaped bottle for whom the whiskey was named, rocking back and forth on the bar top.

"Now, tell us what happened with Parfitt after we left, Bunny. Did you get what you needed?"

He gave us both a very strange look, then shook his head. "I'm not sure you'll believe me if I do."

"What do you mean," I asked.

"It was the damnedest thing, excuse my language."

I smiled, the cultured surroundings were certainly smoothing Bunny's rougher edge.

He took a gulp of his drink then told us what had happened.

"Once you two had got what we needed with regard to the other members of his circle, I asked him about Josephine Brown. If you remember we'd, not very subtly, mentioned his wife and child and then left him?"

Aunt Margaret and I nodded.

"Well, by the time I returned he was in a high state of agitation. Demanding his family be left alone, that they knew nothing and were wholly innocent. Then he reiterated that he was also innocent. So, I played along for a while, then asked him if he was aware Miss Brown was actually one of our agents?

He attempted to look surprised but even I could tell this news wasn't a shock. He knew alright."

"What happened then?" I asked.

"I asked him outright if he'd strangled Miss Brown to death and thrown her body in the Long Water? He denied it, saying he'd never touched her and knew nothing about her death until the police came to visit. Then it all got a bit queer."

"Queer? In what way?" Aunt Margaret asked. "Come along, Bunny, don't drag it out. I'm not getting any younger, you know."

"Alright, you asked for it. Just don't cart me off to the nearest madhouse."

I shared a puzzled look with my aunt. What had happened to cause him such bewilderment?

"Anyway, as soon as he'd denied everything he jumped up and screamed, saying he's just been stabbed in the leg. My man sat him down again, but he was very jumpy from that moment on. I told him we knew he was involved somehow due to the timing of his report on his missing son. He then repeated what he'd said previously, that he knew nothing, and a second later he screamed again and fell from his chair, accusing us of stabbing him in his knee this time."

"Good Lord. How extraordinary. I wonder what..." my aunt broke off and gave me a sharp look. I raised an eyebrow in return. We now had both realised the cause but had to remain silent on the matter.

"Carry on, Bunny," I said.

"He wouldn't sit down after that. Stood against the back wall, eyes darting all over as though waiting for the next attack. I asked him again what he knew and for the third time he said 'nothing,' but it was a half-hearted reply. Unfortunately, another denial resulted in another strike. Back of the calf, and this time I went over to have a look. There were several nasty scratches which had drawn blood. I couldn't explain it. It beggared belief, but I tell you there was something otherworldly at play. All the time I was questioning Parfitt, I'm convinced that room was haunted. Now what do you say about that?"

Yes, what could I say about that? I knew very well the culprit was Phantom, but I could hardly tell Bunny the truth.

"Perhaps you could give us the rest of your report, then we can mull it over?" I said. "I assume he confessed?"

"Oh, yes. Couldn't shut him up after that. The man was terrified out of his wits. And I don't mind telling you I was running a close second."

"And were there any more attacks when he told the truth?"

Bunny eyed me thoughtfully. "No, as a matter of fact, there weren't."

"Well in that case whatever, or whoever..." I amended, as a plan quickly formed in my mind, "was responsible, was obviously there to help you. They were patently on your side, Bunny. Who would want the truth about Miss Brown's murder to be revealed more than you? Who would be prepared to come forth and aid you in such a way? As fantastical as it all sounds, I am a great believer in not only the afterlife but also in a spirit whose earthly form perished before its time wanting their murder to be solved. I believe it allows them to move on."

Bunny stared at me for a second, eyes widening and mouth agape, then he said. "Are you suggesting... I mean do you really think it was... Nightingale? Is that what you're saying? That she came back to help me solve it?"

"I think it's certainly possible, don't you? I mean, how else could you explain what happened?"

"Ella and I are of the same mind here, Bunny," Aunt Margaret said.

"Good heavens," he said softly. "What an exceptional idea. I... it would be marvellous to think she'd been there." He stared into his glass, swirling the amber liquid around as his mind came to terms with what I had suggested. "Just extraordinary," he said. "Comforting too though, actually. Thank you, Miss Bridges."

There was a knock at the door then. Dinner had arrived.

The loaded trolley was wheeled into the room and placed beside the dining table, a waiter standing by ready to serve. My aunt, knowing how confidential our conversation was to be, politely dismissed him with a generous tip, saying we were quite capable of serving ourselves, but they could collect the trolley from the hall later.

Chapter Twelve

OVER DINNER, A MUCH happier Bunny told us what else had transpired during Parfitt's second interrogation. Apparently he had found Miss Brown collecting up his spilled papers from the floor. And while she had made a perfectly feasible excuse-she'd knocked his open briefcase off the table on her way past-Parfitt no longer trusted her.

He'd telephoned the agency from where she'd been hired and demanded a replacement as soon as possible. He'd keep her on until such time a new nanny could be found, he'd said, but an additional week was all he was prepared to give her.

"Well, we know she was one of your agents and not actually a nanny, so who did Parfitt's telephone call get put through to?" I asked.

"A legitimate employment agency," Bunny explained. "But with a designated telephone line handled by one of our female staff." Probably one beginning with a 020 prefix I thought to myself. "Naturally she reported back and plans were put in place to have one of our other girls take Nightingale's place."

"When did this happen?" Aunt Margaret asked.

"Two days before Nightingale was found under the bridge. We obviously haven't replaced her yet."

"Is that all Parfitt did then, report her to the agency?"

Bunny shook his head. "No, he told friends over drinks, apparently. Said he was looking for a new nanny if they could recommend someone. I don't suppose you need me to tell you who those friends were?"

"Batholomew and Arnister?" I said.

"Got it in one. But he swears blind he didn't kill her and didn't know what would happen. His story is he received a telephone call the morning after the drinks conversation, to say the nanny would be dealt with and to await further instructions. He had no idea who telephoned him. Didn't recognise the voice, only to say it was a man, and he had a British accent."

"So, are you saying someone else killed Miss Brown?" I said. "That Parfitt really didn't have anything to do with it?"

"Looks very much like it. Except his idle conversation set the plan in motion. According to Parfitt the second telephone call, the next day, informed him where his son could be found and that the nanny was no longer a problem. He had no idea at that point she'd been killed. Of course, you know what happened next."

"I took the baby home."

"But that doesn't explain how he knew Josephine Brown was an intelligence agent," Aunt Margaret said. "From what you've told us when you interrogated him, it was obvious he knew then, as you said you could tell he was lying. Yet his previous actions lead me to believe he wasn't aware. But due to his own complicity and guilt decided he had to get rid of her just in case she'd seen something she shouldn't within his spilled papers. Even if it would have meant nothing to her."

"Spot on, Snow White, as usual. He was told after the fact. During the second telephone call. He was stunned as you can imagine. She'd been in his employ for a year and a half at that point and he had no inkling she was a spy herself. Makes him look like a complete and utter fool though in my opinion."

"Ah, I see now."

"We still need to find whoever is responsible for the murder though," I said, between mouthfuls of lemon sole and new potatoes.

"We will, Miss Bridges." Bunny said patting my hand. "Especially if Josephine is helping us."

———— ◉ ————

OVER DESSERT OF CRÈME brûlée with fresh raspberries Bunny put forth his plan.

In the days since we'd last seen him, he'd done a considerable amount of work looking into the backgrounds and lives of Parfitt's partners in crime and decided Edward Batholomew was the better of the two to target personally.

"Why not Arnister as well?" my aunt asked. "He could be my mark. He's a member of the Athenaeum club, if I remember correctly?"

"Yes, but you're a woman."

"Fabulous powers of observation as per usual, Bunny."

"Oh, very witty, Snow. You know what I mean. It's a men's club. They won't let you in."

"As a matter of fact, earlier this year they did just that. They extended into Gladstone's house, made it into a ladies' annexe and we're allowed to attend with a member. They have a dining room *and* a drawing room, Bunny. Imagine!"

I laughed at my aunt's sarcasm and Bunny shook his head.

"One day I shall get the better of you, you know."

"Well, today is not that day. Now, how about it? Can I infiltrate this club for the good of our Empire or not?"

"Let me give it some thought. I agree attacking from more than one direction makes sense, but I'm not promising anything. We'll discuss it later."

"Of course, dear man. Now, what was your idea? Ella going undercover, I assume?"

"How do you know?" I asked.

"Because your aunt has already been in Parfitt's employ once at the Foreign Office and her face, well one of them at least, is already known."

"You have more than one face, Aunt Margaret? Where do you keep the others, in a box under the bed?" I asked with a grin.

"Nowhere so obvious, dear," she said with a grin that mirrored my own. "They're in a safety deposit box at the bank."

I burst out laughing at that and she joined me. It was wonderful to be able to see the humourous side of things again. My foray into the bunkers of the Secret Intelligence Service had cast a pall of darkness which had threatened to overcome me completely. It was a relief to feel it lifting, to be able to see the light and to finally have something useful to do. When all this was over I vowed to learn as much as I could from my aunt. Her secret past was now well and truly out in the open. I may as well take advantage of it and add some new skills to my repertoire.

After a few minutes of indulging us and joining in with the laughter, Bunny asked if we could get on with the plan.

"Of course, carry on," Aunt Margaret said.

"So, Batholomew's secretary handed her notice in the day before yesterday..."

"Why?" I asked.

"Well, if you give me a chance I shall explain. Snow, would you be so kind as to pour me another coffee? I feel as though I need to keep my wits about me. Talking to your niece is like having a conversation with a younger version of you. The reason being, Miss Bridges, is that she has found better employ elsewhere. Yes, we instigated it and found her a new position, but she was on the verge of leaving, anyway. Batholomew is a notoriously difficult man to work for. He's short-tempered, doesn't suffer fools gladly and can't abide clever women. She'd had enough. While she's a smart girl and very efficient, she isn't strong emotionally."

"Oh, dear. You'd better 'dumb it down' as I believe they say in Hollywood, Ella. You're as sharp as a Porcupine Quill and won't last two minutes if he realises how bright you are."

"I agree with your Aunt. And it wouldn't do you any harm to develop a thick skin while you're at it."

"Don't worry about me, I have a hide like a rhinoceros. So, I'm to be his secretary?"

"His personal assistant is the correct title, I believe."

"Alright, I'll do it. So, I start at the newspaper offices in Bouverie Street, just off Fleet Street, isn't it? the day after to-morrow. What are my duties to be?"

"Well, naturally there are two sets of duties, one for him and one for us. You're only a temp from the agency, remember, but you'll need to be in the position for as long as it takes for you to find what we need. You'll help him with the filing, typing, writing up his letters; he'll dictate those for you, and anything else that he requires. Within reason of course. But I daresay he'll ask you to run errands such as getting him cigarettes or making him coffee."

"I'm sure I can manage those."

"As for the SIS, we'll need to see all his correspondence so you'll need to ensure you're the one who takes them to the post. There's a central area where it's left for a runner who takes them to the post office. However, you'll keep Batholomew's on you and pass them onto your contact every evening when you leave. I'll give you further instructions on how and where when it's all confirmed. With me so far?"

"Yes. Who do you have in mind for my contact? I'd prefer it to be someone I'm already familiar with."

I thought back to the traumatic motor car journey in the company of two strangers. I wasn't going to make that mistake again.

"How about Carstairs, will he do?"

"Admirably. Thank you. So, what happens to the post when I pass it on?"

"It will be taken to a SIS location nearby where it will be carefully opened, copied and studied. Once that has been done, it will be resealed and returned to the post office where it will become part of the system, delivered as planned and with neither Batholomew nor his intended recipient being any the wiser."

"With you so far. Is there anything else?"

"Yes. His telephone calls. More difficult, I'm afraid, as you'll be situated outside his private office, but take notes on everything you hear. You never know, something seemingly innocuous could in fact be very important. Just keep your eyes and ears open for anything else you think we should know, whether it be from Batholomew himself or one of his colleagues. Or another of the support staff for that matter. I suspect the place is the same as any other large organisation, a hotbed of gossip. Finally, do not take any risks. I can't stress enough how dangerous these people are. We've already lost one of our colleagues. I don't want to lose another. If you feel your cover has been compromised, drop everything and leave. Immediately! Your safety is the most important thing."

"Yes, I understand. I have no intention of putting myself in any danger. But what if I discover something important which needs relaying quickly? How do I contact you?"

"You'll be given a code word to use and a telephone number. There's a telephone on your desk so it should be easy enough."

I nodded. "Let's make it something sensible, shall we? That wouldn't sound too out of place in an office or on a personal call from work?"

He laughed. "Yes alright. I'll leave it with you. Now, I really must be getting on. Do you have any other questions before I leave?"

"No, I have everything, thank you."

"Thank you, Miss Bridges. I realise we are putting a lot on your shoulders but we're spread a bit thin with regard to the female staff at present."

"Don't worry, Bunny. I've done it before. But perhaps you should have a recruitment drive, I'm sure there are a lot of highly qualified women out there who would jump at the chance to do this sort of work."

"Perhaps you're right. I'll certainly ponder the options. Thank you both for a wonderful meal and the pleasure of your company. It's been an education."

"Good night, Bunny," Aunt Margaret said. "Once this is all over we'll do it again." She showed him out while I walked behind, pushing the dinner trolley into the hall for collection.

Once Bunny had left Aunt Margaret and I decided to have a nightcap before retiring. She handed me a brandy before settling down beside me on the settee.

"I must say that part about Nightingale's spirit being in the room while he was questioning Parfitt was inspired, Ella. I could see the weight lift from his shoulders. He went away a different man. Did you believe it?"

"It's highly possible. We know Phantom was there in the room as I saw him before Parfitt was questioned for the first time. And I know he was the one responsible for the scratches, he's an extraordinarily clever creature. But I've seen Miss Brown twice now, and the second time Phantom was with her. So who's to say she didn't appear after we'd left and Phantom and she worked together? I'm just glad Bunny has found some measure of peace."

"And you've found a new job, darling. Do let me know if you need some help brushing up on your skills, won't you?"

"Touché, Aunt Margaret. But my skills in that regard are just fine. However, we'll need the dressing-up box, I think."

"Jolly good job I brought it with me then, isn't it? And before you ask, yes, that is hidden under the bed."

Chapter Thirteen

ON WEDNESDAY MORNING I was up early ready to begin my first day at The News Chronicle.

The previous day my aunt and I had rummaged through her disguise paraphernalia and decided on a suitable outfit. It was a plain skirt suit in drab Olive green, terribly frumpy and dated but it did the trick. I'd also opted for a pair of spectacles with clear lenses.

I'd said no to the blond wig and positively balked at the false nose which my aunt had thrust toward me with a giggle, settling instead for some light cosmetics. For one who very rarely wore make-up of any kind the results of darkened eyebrows, rouged cheeks and a slash of coral lipstick rendered me quite unrecognisable.

My aunt also pinned my hair back and gave me a tight black cloche hat, which made me look as though I had a coal scuttle on my head.

"Yes, I think this will do, don't you?" I said, scrutinising my reflection in my aunt's dressing-room mirror.

"Absolutely. You look just like a Murial."

Murial Simpkins was to be my name for a while so I needed to get used to it.

Bunny had called the previous day to confirm everything was in place. The letters which I typed for Batholomew myself wouldn't need the scrutiny of the SIS team, unless the information was deemed of interest, in which case I would pass on the details verbally either to Carstairs or via telephone later. Those could go into the post collection box for the paper's runner to deal with. The rest I would pass to Carstairs on the No. 15 bus, which I would get on at Chancery Lane and ride to Oxford Circus, a journey of fifteen minutes. From there, I could walk the five minute distance back to Claridges.

For my first day I ordered a taxi to take me to Whitefriars Street. It was the road off Fleet Street which ran parallel to Bouverie Street so was within easy walking distance. A moment later I pushed open the heavy double doors and entered the reception area.

"Can I help you?" the woman behind the counter asked.

"Yes. I'm Murial Simpkins. I'm due to start as Mr Batholomew's secretary today."

"Sign in, please," she said, sliding a large book across the counter top. "I'll tell Mrs Huntley you're here."

I did as she asked while she announced my arrival.

"Have a seat, Miss Simpkins. Mrs Huntley is on her way."

A clip clopping of heels down the stairs a few moments later signalled her arrival.

"Miss Simpkins, please follow me."

She was a tall, slim and quite manly-looking woman of middle age, with iron grey hair cut short. Her back was ramrod straight, and she gave off an aura of absolute authority that brooked no argument. As she escorted me to my new office, she didn't so much talk as give me a list of instructions.

"You may work for Mr Batholomew but you answer to me, do you understand? Your working day begins at eight o'clock promptly and I expect you to be at your desk and ready to begin at that time. It ends at half-past five unless Mr Batholomew needs you to stay later. Although that is rare it has been known. You will have three quarters of an hour for lunch and be back at your desk no later than a quarter past one. If your duties take you over into your lunch break, then you will forfeit that time. While we have a staff canteen on the lower floor, I suggest bringing a packed lunch which you can eat at your desk. Mr Batholomew is a very busy man and in all likelihood he will require you to work at a moment's notice, this will include during your breaks. Remember your time is not your own, Miss Simpkins, it belongs to the company, to me and to Mr Batholomew."

We'd reached the upper floor and walked to the end of a corridor where she entered an outer office with a desk, chair, filing cabinet and two large cupboards. She opened one and pointed.

"You can hang your coat and hat in here. Well, come along, I haven't got all day."

I hurriedly shed my coat and hung it up. Unpinning my hat, I laid it on a shelf above the hanging rail along with my handbag.

"This is the stationary cupboard," she said, opening the second large cupboard. "As you can see it contains everything you will need to do your job, but if paper or envelopes are wasted unnecessarily the cost of replacement will be deducted from your wage. Understood? This is your desk with telephone and typewriter. I assume you know how to use both? Under no circumstances other than an absolute emergency are you to use the telephone for personal reasons. In the drawers you will find notepads and pens and anything else you may require. Again, these are the property of the company and under no circumstances are they to be used for personal use, or taken off the premises. Do you understand? If Mr Batholomew requires your assistance, he will telephone you. Answer it, then go through to his office, immediately. Some incoming calls for him are also put through here. You'll need to confirm he wishes to speak to the caller prior to transferring it through to his telephone. Do you understand?"

I'd given up trying to answer every time she asked me that as she didn't give me a chance, nor I suspect did she expect me to. I either understood or I didn't and if I didn't then I would soon get my marching orders. She briefly showed me how the telephone worked, then with an about turn she bid me good morning and left.

I dropped into my chair with relief at her departure. "Good Lord, what a tartar," I mumbled. Then the telephone rang. It was from Mr Batholomew's office. Time to get to work.

———————◉———————

"HELLO?"

"Patty, get in here. I need a letter writing."

I had no chance to answer before he put the receiver down, so I gathered my notepad and pen and hurried into his office. He was standing with his back to the door looking out of the window.

"Take this down, will you? Dear Mr Struthers, judging from our recent conversation..." He turned then and saw me still standing in the middle of the room.

"Who the hell are you?"

What a charming greeting. I looked into cold blue eyes set into a long horse-like face with a prominent nose which ended in a pointed chin below a cruel mouth. I schooled my features into a bland look and answered.

"Murial Simpkins, Mr Batholomew. I'm your new secretary."

"Oh God, not another one. What happened to what's her name, Patty?"

"She left, sir."

"Well of course she bally well left... oh never mind, you're all ten-a-penny, anyway. Let's get on with it, shall we?"

I sat and took down the letter in shorthand, reading it back when asked to and remaining quiet until I was asked a direct question.

"Right, that'll do. Type it up and bring it back."

I left his office and, feeding a new sheet of paper into the typewriter, had it completed quickly, and with a sharp knock on the door, entered and laid it on his desk, then waited. Scrawling his signature he pushed it back at me.

"Out in the post tonight, Patty. And get this typed up." He thrust several sheets of paper at me all covered in writing. I glanced at it quickly and was relieved to see it was legible.

"It's Murial, sir."

"What's Murial?"

"My name."

"Right. Off you go then."

The morning carried on in much the same vein. I was called to take dictation and type up the responses, all the while being called Patty. I'd given up correcting him; he knew it wasn't my name yet insisted on using it. It was obviously some sort of power play, but considering my name wasn't Murial either I could just as easily answer to something else.

At a quarter past twelve he left the office saying he would return at some point in the afternoon. This was a relief as it meant I could go and find the canteen and get some lunch.

At three o'clock he returned and more letters and typing continued. I put the odd telephone call through but in the main callers were transferred directly to his own office line via the company switchboard. I gleaned nothing from them as his office door remained tightly shut.

At twenty-five past five he reappeared dressed for the outdoors and threw two sealed and addressed envelopes for me to take to the post area. At the door to my office, he turned and gave me a sharp look.

"Get in early tomorrow, Patty. Lots to do." Then he turned on his heel and left.

I sighed with relief. My first day was over and it had been utterly horrible. Bunny's description of the man had been woefully underestimated. Edward Batholomew was an out-and-out monster.

———— ◉ ————

I LEFT THE OFFICE AT exactly five-thirty and trotted down the stairs feeling lighter with every step. I signed out at the reception desk and made my way down Bouverie Street turning left at the bottom onto Fleet Street.

Several yards on, I crossed over the road onto Chancery Lane and walked past the Bank of England. A beautiful building built fifty years previously in a grand Italianate style, with three huge chandeliers inside hanging from an ornate plasterwork ceiling. The vaults were filled with gold bullion and I wondered if I was walking on top of one of England's many treasures as I made my way to the bus stop.

There were quite a few people waiting when I arrived, and even more on the No. 15 bus itself. I managed to find a seat midway but saw no sign of Carstairs.

Two stops later, Carstairs got on and several people exited, leaving the seat behind me free. I'd picked up the letters Batholomew had written himself, and as per instructions was now sitting on them. Once I got up to exit at my Oxford Circus stop Carstairs rose too and took my place. I'd left the letters for him on the seat. During the exchange we didn't acknowledge one another but as the bus pulled away, I caught his eye through the window and he gave me a quick wink.

By a quarter past six I had divested myself of 'Murial' and was seated in the living room of our suite drinking a much needed cup of tea.

"Dare I ask how your day was, darling?" Aunt Margaret said.

"The work itself was easy, enjoyable in fact, but Batholomew himself? Good Lord, Aunt Margaret, why on earth do some people feel the need to be so nasty? He is absolutely dreadful, inflated to the point of bursting with self-importance, and I for one can't wait for him to get his just deserts. The man has a face like a horse and acts like the other end of one. And Mrs Huntley, my supervisor, is just as bad. An absolute harridan if ever there was one. It's no wonder poor Patty wanted to leave. I'm surprised they have any secretaries there at all."

"Oh dear, I am sorry, Ella. But look on the bright side. It's only very temporary. The best thing is to keep your head down and remain quiet and efficient and don't draw attention to yourself. Blend into the very walls, dear, that's the ticket."

I smiled. "I have become a paragon of dutifulness and docility, Aunt Margaret. I shall continue to slave away for the greater good."

"I'm glad you've got your sense of humour, Ella. Very important in times of stress. So, did you get anything to Carstairs?"

"Yes, a couple of letters. Let's hope there's something in them so I can inform Huntley I'm leaving."

Unfortunately, nothing was found, so bright and early on Thursday morning, I was back at my desk. Although this time I did bring a lunch with me courtesy of Claridges' kitchen.

⸻ ◉ ⸻

THE REMAINDER OF MY working week continued in much the same way and I found myself silently praying for Bunny's men to find something quickly in the pilfered correspondence, for I didn't know how much longer I could keep going.

It had only been three days, but it felt like a lifetime. Edward Batholomew was a rude, self-centered, bombastic and insufferable individual who got worse and worse as time went on. I would relish giving him a piece of my mind and consequently spent a fair amount of time daydreaming of such an occurrence. My only solace was the fact I knew who he really was, a traitor and quite possibly a murderer, and soon would get his come-uppance.

On Friday evening I left with Batholomew's private correspondence and once again Carstairs took possession of them

on the bus. Thankfully I wasn't expected to work on the week-
ends, so I had two whole days of peace to look forward to. Then
at eight o'clock the telephone rang. It was Bunny. Apparently,
even with his best men on the job, nothing had been found. He
was requesting our help.

At nine o'clock, Aunt Margaret and I were once again
guests in the Secret Intelligence Service's bunker room under St
James' Park. This time I didn't mind so much. It was certainly
preferable to being at the newspaper offices, even if there were
no windows.

Several wall heaters also supplied a modicum of heat and
combined with the natural warmth of the other people present,
it was actually quite pleasant. I nodded to Carstairs who was
overseeing the work of a team on the other side of the room.

"Tell me what you've done so far, Bunny?" Aunt Margaret
asked, as we looked at the letters spread out on a central desk.

"Everything has been copied in triplicate and each team has
worked on a copy looking for every code or cipher we know of.
There's nothing."

"This includes the envelopes?" I asked, watching Phantom
sitting proudly on top of one.

"Of course. Same story, nothing. We've even looked for mi-
crodots within and under the stamps. There has to be something, but whatever it is, I'm damned if I can find it!"

"Well, we'd better get to it then," my aunt said, metaphori-
cally rolling up her sleeves.

We sat together at the central table and began sifting
through the originals, notepads at our sides as we scribbled and
worked our way through every code and cipher we were familiar with. Being familiar with this type of work, my aunt knew

more than I did, but showed me how they worked and what to look for. Before long I felt as though I could hold my own against the best of them.

Several hours and numerous cups of coffee later we were on the verge of admitting defeat, when I suddenly thought of my father.

When the business had been going well and my father had been in a playful mood, he had a particular parlour trick which Gerry and I loved. We'd spent hours working out the various clues in the notes he left us, each one leading to another then finally to a prize at the end. Usually sweets. Could it really be that simple? We'd been focusing purely on complicated mechanisms because the more intricate the problem the more difficult they were to break. Perhaps it was a bluff? The other side would expect us to do exactly what we had done, namely spend hours tying ourselves into a Gordian knot.

I glanced up to find Phantom had moved and was sat staring at one of the heaters. This reinforced my belief we were looking for something so simple we'd never given it credence.

"Do you mind?" I asked Bunny, indicating the envelope Phantom had been sitting on when we'd arrived hours previously. It had been addressed to Arnister.

"Help yourself."

I took the envelope, then followed Phantom to the heater plugged into the wall. As I held it over the heat, a message appeared.

"Oh, well done, Ella!" Aunt Margaret cried. "Whatever gave you that idea?"

"I suddenly thought of the games Father used to set up for us. That and more than a little help from my old cat," I finished with a whisper.

"Of all the simple things! Secret writing!" Bunny cried in frustration. He glared at his staff, all of whom had stopped what they were doing, sensing a tirade. They weren't wrong. "What the hell is this, amateur hour? You're supposed to be the brightest and the best, yet you can't even figure out the simplest clue there is. You should be ashamed of yourselves."

"Sometimes the simplest ideas are the best," I said, handing him the envelope, and trying to calm him down. "We did exactly what they expected us to, Bunny. Worked through the most difficult ciphers and came up blank, wasting time in the process. I hate to admit it, but it was rather a clever idea to do something a child would be familiar with. As adults we no longer think with the innocence of children, as life in reality is complicated. But it's done. I suggest we move on and put it down to experience and learn from it."

Bunny gave a curt nod. "I'm still not happy. But I'll deal with it later."

"Please, do remember your team has been working around the clock for the last few days, Bunny. They are tired and frustrated too. It's easy to make mistakes when you are at your lowest."

"Alright, you've made your point, Miss Bridges," he replied in quieter tones, then turned back to his team. "Right, let's get to work and check everything again," he ordered his teams, who at once scrambled for the original documents and dashed to the various heaters. "We've already missed the last few days' worth now they're back in the postal system. I'm not prepared to miss anything else. If there's something there I want it found."

"What does it say?" my aunt asked, once Bunny stopped to draw breath.

"It's not good news, Snow. Looks like we've run out of time."

Chapter Fourteen

"FOUND SOMETHING, SIR," came a call from the other side of the room and one of Bunny's team hurried over with a sheet of paper. There, in the left-hand-side margin of the banal letter inside the envelope was the same message.

New sec. a plant.
Exit initiated.
48 hours.
Use established protocols.
Details to follow.

"Right," Bunny said. "Get this lot back together and deliver it to our man at the post office. It needs to be back in the system so they don't suspect anything."

"Yes, Sir."

The man hurried off, shouting instructions, while the three of us moved to Bunny's office.

"Disappointingly, it's obvious the first line means me," I said. "But I am almost positive I wasn't followed. I was extremely careful. How did he know? What did I do wrong that gave me away?"

"It might not have been you, Ella. It could be something as simple as him being suspicious of every newcomer into his life and checking them out. I expect they've all been in a state of high alert ever since Josephine Brown's murder. Having Scotland Yard poking around will do that."

"But they mention me specifically, Aunt Margaret."

"Indeed. But expanding on my previous statement, in all likelihood they were being careful and watching *all* new people, not just you. If you had been followed, for instance, and it would be possible with someone you'd not seen before no matter how careful you were, then they could have seen you pass the post to Carstairs. And if they missed that, then the fact that a lowly secretary was living in a suite at Claridges most certainly would raise alarms. I think we must face facts, with them knowing Parfitt's been arrested they were being extra vigilant and found what they were looking for."

"Me."

"Yes, you. And now they've set in motion their planned extraction."

"This letter though," I said holding up the paper from the envelope. "It's written to Parfitt. Why would Batholomew write to him if he knows he's been caught?"

"It could be a double bluff," said Bunny, scratching his chin. "Something to trap us, perhaps? Or it could be that they genuinely don't know we've got him. Parfitt, Batholomew and Arnister could all have their own contacts, they're all passing on different types of information after all. Just because Parfitt's contact didn't pick up what was left for him at the church doesn't mean the others know. Perhaps it's as simple as the left hand deliberately not knowing what the right is doing? It protects everybody. But it's all supposition and conjecture, and quite frankly it's the least of our problems. According to this missive we only have forty-eight hours in which to catch them or we'll lose them for good."

"But we have no idea what their exit plan is," I said.

"We are both now free to work on it, Ella. Such a shame I won't be needed to infiltrate the Athenaeum Club though. I was rather looking forward to it."

"I, on the other hand am thrilled I won't have to set foot in The News Chronicle offices again."

"I doubt it will matter, dear. Edward Batholomew is likely lying low now until he can leave, so it's probable he'll not be there either come Monday morning. They'll probably think you ran off together."

"Aunt Margaret! What an appalling thought. Bunny, please ensure someone informs Mrs Huntley that I will not be returning to work. Tell them my aunt is gravely ill."

Aunt Margaret laughed then turned to Bunny. "I assume they're defecting to Russia?"

"Yes, that'll be the place to start. They'll need an aeroplane. I'll arrange surveillance at the airports and private airfields, but I'll need additional manpower to cover them all. I wonder if Scotland Yard could assist?" Bunny said, looking at me.

"I'll telephone Baxter tomorrow, it's too late now, and see if he can organise something. I haven't spoken to him since we all met at the London Library. I'd rather hoped he'd have been in touch before now."

"Something wrong?"

"I'm not sure but I think so. He's not been himself recently, so I deliberately took a step back in order for him to be alone and work things through for himself. Now, I'm not sure it was such a good idea. I do hope he doesn't think I've abandoned him."

"Of course he won't, Ella. Baxter is a good man but like all men he's not terribly good at talking about feelings," Aunt

Margaret said with a stern glance at Bunny. "He'll come round, you'll see, and I expect he'll be glad of the opportunity to help. Now, Bunny, this last line, 'details to follow,' is most likely to be the time and place for the final meeting, in which case there must be some sort of signal. But how do we find it? They won't use the post method again, it will take too long. Have you still got agents following Arnister and Batholomew?"

"Yes, they check in regularly but nothing untoward so far. However, in light of what we've just discovered, I'll let them know to be extra vigilant and report back more frequently."

"If it's a signal we're looking for, there's only one person we can ask who knows what it could be," I said.

"Parfitt," Aunt Margaret and Bunny said together.

I nodded. "We need to go back and talk to him."

"Well, we're in luck because we just had to move him. That spirit terrified the life out of him and he spent much of the time afterward screaming and demanding to be moved. He's here at a safe house in London."

———— ◉ ————

AUNT MARGARET DISAPPEARED into Bunny's office to make a telephone call before we set off to speak to James Parfitt. I had no idea who she called at such an unearthly hour, but she asked for a short stop at Claridges before we continued our journey.

Bunny was driving this time, and I was sat in the rear of the motor car watching the entrance to the hotel when Aunt Margaret reappeared, swinging a large picnic hamper. She passed it through to me, then got in the front.

"Thank you, Bunny, we can go now."

"What is all this, Aunt Margaret?" I asked opening the lid.

"We missed dinner, darling, and I simply can't think on an empty stomach. Claridges are wonderful and have a twenty-four-hour service for the whims of their clientele."

"Enough for three is there, Snow?"

"Of course there is, Bunny."

"In that case I'll forgive the twenty minute detour you've brought me on."

"Oh, have I really? Well, thank you for not letting me fade away to nothing, Bunny. Now, Ella, be a dear and pass me a sandwich, would you?"

And that's how we spent the ten-minute journey, munching on a superlative selection of Claridges' goodies.

Bunny took Brook Street and Hanover Square to Cavendish Square, then a few yards on turned right onto the A5204 then left onto Nassau Street in Fitzrovia, our destination.

The street was a single row of four-storey houses, built in red brick with cream lintels and bay windows on the ground floor. There were no gardens to speak of and they were all fronted with tall, black iron railings and matching gates.

We entered the least well-kept of them all at the very end of the row, but as I'd come to realise looks can be deceiving and inside, it was elegant and immaculate, though obviously uninhabited. We were met in the hallway by Carstairs, who thanks to my Aunt's detour had beaten us to the house.

"Everything alright?" asked Bunny.

"Yes, sir. He's waiting for you. I brought Brookes with me from the office to relieve the other guard."

Carstairs led us through to the kitchen at the back of the house where he unlocked a door leading to the cellar. We followed down stone steps into a sparse, whitewashed area consisting of two rooms and a small WC. Parfitt was sitting at an old deal table with one of the SIS men acting as guard. He looked thin and exhausted but his clothes were fresh and the bruising on his face had mellowed to shades of ochre and violet, tinged with green.

He looked up as we entered and his eyes lit on me. "You?" he spat with a malevolence which startled me. But in hindsight I shouldn't have been surprised. This whole thing had started by me finding his son. I ignored him and followed Aunt Margaret.

At a nod from Carstairs, Brookes rose and headed upstairs and Bunny took his place. Carstairs stood behind him and Aunt Margaret and I sat at what was once a church pew at the far side of the room.

"Bad news, Parfitt," Bunny began. "Your comrades are hanging you out to dry. In less than forty-eight hours they've got plans to leave the country."

Parfitt's eyes widened momentarily then he frowned. "I don't believe you."

"No? Well, have a look at this," Bunny extracted from an inside pocket the letter and envelope that Batholomew had penned to Arnister, the secret message we'd revealed in the margin, and slid it across the table.

Parfitt scanned the contents, his expression turning to horror and anger, then finally bitterness tinged with acceptance as the reality of his predicament sunk in. He thrust the letter back.

"I can't help you."

"Think again," Bunny replied, his voice tinged with steel.

"What difference will it make? I'll be tried for treason whether I help you or not."

"Ah, well, that's where you're wrong you see. Standing trial would be the best outcome for you, granted, but I doubt you'll ever see the inside of a courtroom."

Parfitt gasped. "What do you mean? I'm entitled to a fair trial. You'd never get away with it!"

"Wrong again, I'm afraid. Do you think the Government want it plastered all over the newspapers that they had a Russian agent working in the Foreign Office? Don't be a fool, man, they want this all to go away nice and quietly. And I'm the perfect man for the job."

"You can't! I have rights."

"Rights!" Bunny roared, launching himself up and leaning menacingly over the table towards Parfitt, inches from his face as he continued to yell. "You squandered your rights when you started to give away the nation's secrets to our enemy! You have nothing, least of all rights. Let's face it, you're up the proverbial creek without a paddle."

"What do you want from me?"

"I want to know what the protocols for your exit plan are. What are the details Batholomew mentions in his note to Arnister?"

Parfitt shook his head. "I can't, they'll kill me."

"Well, son, they'll have to get in line." Bunny resumed his seat and rubbed a hand over his head, sighing. "Look at the facts, Parfitt. Who, out of the three of you have the most to lose? Got families have they, Arnister and Batholomew? No, didn't think so. You on the other hand have a small son and a doting wife. What do you think will happen to them now? Your wife will be shunned by society for having a traitor as a husband, that's if she isn't proved to be a spy herself. And your son will grow up without a father at the very least, or as an orphan. Both of them ostracised and no matter how far they go your foul deeds will follow them. Your pals don't give a hoot about you and yours, they're out to save their own skins and you're more of a fool than I took you for if you think otherwise. They killed your nanny, for God's sake and left you to take the blame."

"Elizabeth is innocent. She knows nothing, I swear. And Rupert is just a baby, he needs his mother. Please, promise me they'll be left alone and I'll help you."

Bunny sat back, folding his arms and watching Parfitt carefully for a moment. Then he turned and looked at Aunt Margaret, at me, then returned his gaze to Parfitt as though thinking seriously about his request. In reality, Elizabeth Parfitt had been told her husband was away on business for the Foreign Office. Letters, written by the SIS on behalf of her husband, had already been received by her and she was none the wiser as to what was really going on. But James Parfitt, of course, didn't know any of this. Eventually Bunny unfolded his arms and nodded.

"Alright, I'll make that promise, but only when you've told me everything and I have proof."

Parfitt sighed. "I'll tell you what I know, but it's not much. A chalk mark on a lamppost in Audley Square is the signal that an immediate extraction is needed. Edward is the one in charge of doing that and then he contacts us to confirm. If you've got his letter, then it's already been done. If Edward has been compromised, then it's Richard's job."

"What happens after that?"

"I would receive a telephone call from one or the other, inviting me for a drink on a certain day and time at the club..."

"The Athenaeum?"

There was a pause as Parfitt realised how far we'd come in our investigation, then he confirmed it.

"Yes. The date and time are actually the details for the meetup where we proceed to leave the country."

"Where would you meet?"

"I don't know. Someone would contact me."

"Arnister or Batholomew?"

"No, I don't think so. It would be another contact but I don't know who, and it would be at the last minute for security. That's all I know. I swear to God."

Bunny stood up and indicated Aunt Margaret and I should follow. Carstairs was to remain with Parfitt.

This would be where we needed to confirm what he had told us.

———————⬤———————

IN THE UPSTAIRS KITCHEN Bunny had a quick word with Brookes who was sitting at a small table drinking a cup of coffee.

"Get yourself over to Audley Square immediately," he said, handing Brookes the keys to the motor car. "There's an old Victorian lamppost in the square, just off South Audley Street. It's not really a square, more a small enclave."

"I know the one, Sir. It stands outside the University Women's Club. What am I looking for?"

"A chalk mark on the lamppost, probably somewhere near ground level. Keep your eyes peeled. It could be under observation. Look for anything else suspicious too."

"Right, Sir. On my way. If all goes well I'll be back in about half an hour."

Once his man had left Bunny turned to us and asked us if Parfitt was telling the truth.

"Yes," I said. "He doesn't know as much as we thought, but what he's told you is the truth as far as he knows it."

"I agree," Aunt Margaret said. "But there seems to be a step missing. According to Parfitt, Batholomew puts a chalk mark on the lamppost and writes to his cohorts confirming, then he calls them later with the date and time. What happens in between? Who gives Batholomew the date and time for the meeting?"

"Parfitt won't know that," Bunny said. "I get the feeling he's the more junior of the three, no matter what his ego tells him, and he's given us what he knows. But you do have a point."

"Is it worth letting Parfitt go and seeing if they make contact with him?" I said.

"The last thing I want to do is let that turncoat go. It's a big risk, considering they most likely know he's been talking to us. Let's wait until my man is back before we make any such decisions." He glanced at his watch. "Shouldn't be too long now. If he finds something then that will dictate our next steps. Assuming it's a go, we should hopefully be able to follow and catch them before they leave our shores, ideally after they meet their Russian contact. I'd like to catch that blighter too."

While we were waiting for Bunny's agent to return we drank the tea and ate the remaining contents of the hamper. I stifled a yawn and glanced at my aunt who was also fighting to remain awake. Bunny on the other hand was filled with adrenaline and was pacing like a caged tiger.

Eventually at nearly a quarter to four in the morning we heard the front door slam and hurried footsteps coming down the hall.

"Anything?" Bunny barked before the man could speak.

"Yes, Sir. The chalk mark's there alright. But it's also a cunning dead drop, and I found something else."

"WELL, WHAT HAVE YOU got, Brookes?"

Brookes took his notebook from his pocket and turned to a page, "There was a note cleverly concealed in a trapdoor at the back of the lamppost. I copied it out, Sir."

"What? You didn't bring it back with you? There could have been secret writing on it, man."

"There wasn't, sir." Brookes replied unperturbed at his superior's outburst. He dug a hand in his pocket and brought out a box of matches. "I was in the office when the secret messages were found on the envelope and letter. I checked and there was nothing there."

"Well done, Brookes. My apologies. Carry on."

He tore the page from the notebook and handed it to Bunny. "This is it in its entirety. Copied faithfully but I'm afraid it's in code again, sir."

Bunny sighed heavily and handed the page to my aunt, who after a quick glance handed it on to me. It was just a series of lines and dots, some full squares with nothing inside, some with a dot to the right, left or middle. I'd never seen anything like it before and couldn't see how we would be able to crack it.

"What on earth is it?" I asked.

Aunt Margaret was hurriedly scribbling in her notebook, first a copy of the original message, then lines like a noughts and crosses board with a section of the alphabet above each set of squares and dots, left, middle and centre. When she'd been working for no more than five minutes, she threw her pen down in disgust.

"It's not breakable without a keyword, Bunny."

"Blast it!"

"What is it, Aunt Margaret?"

"It's a Rosicrucian Cipher, Ella. Also known as a Pigpen, Masonic, Freemason or Napoleon cipher. It's a relatively simple geometric substitution cipher, exchanging letters for symbols which are fragments of a grid. But this one has a twist. It's gone one step further and has, to the best of my knowledge, based it on an initial keyword which governs the start letter of the alphabet. It won't work otherwise."

"So, you mean rather than writing the alphabet from A to Z, it could start in the middle, from N or P for example?"

"That's right. But without the keyword which will tell us what letter to start it from we can't work out what the message says. In fact, it may not actually use the whole alphabet but only a partial section repeated. The permutations are countless. And that's not to say it couldn't be an entire phrase rather than a single code word, and that would be nearly impossible to break. I'm sorry, Bunny, but it's after four in the morning and I am suffering from chronic fatigue. Long gone are the days when I could remain awake from dawn to dawn with no ill effects. I can't possibly work on this now. Ella and I will make copies and begin again in the morning."

"Of course, thank you both and apologies for it being such a late night. I'll have Carstairs run you back to Claridges. In the meantime, I'll set the team working on this new code to see if we can break it."

"It can't be done, Bunny. Not without the key word or phrase."

"Maybe, but I have to try, Snow. God help us all if they're allowed to escape. Get a good rest and we'll speak again tomorrow."

We returned to our hotel bone weary and with a sense of despondency. All the work we'd put into the case so far and we were thwarted at the eleventh hour!

Chapter Fifteen

I MANAGED JUST OVER five hours' sleep and was up and ready to begin the day by half past ten, albeit with a slight headache. My aunt shuffled in a quarter of an hour later and we ate a quiet breakfast together before I put a telephone call through to Baxter.

"Good morning, Miss Bridges, this is a surprise."

"Hello, Baxter, how are you?"

"Being kept busy with several cases, theft and arson mostly. You?"

"Still on the same case actually, but it's taken a rather serious turn and Bunny needs your assistance."

I gave him a brief report of the case to date, culminating in the need for additional men to keep an eye on the airports and airfields surrounding London.

"That's a lot of men, Miss Bridges. But I'll see what I can do."

"Thank you, Baxter. I do appreciate your help."

"You're welcome. Is there anything else I can help with?"

I rubbed my temple as the headache began to worsen. "No, I think that's it for now. I'll speak to you again soon."

"Alright, goodbye for now."

I wandered back into the living room where Aunt Margaret looked at me with concern.

"Are you alright, Ella?"

"Bit of a headache, that's all."

"I've got some Beecham's Pills somewhere that will do the trick. Let me get them for you."

"Oh, I've heard of those. Quite recently I think..." Now where had I heard them mentioned before?

I stood stock still in the middle of the room while my mind hunted for their mention. Smoke Balls! The dame and Bunny's shock at the news of Miss Brown's death when he shouldn't have been so!

"Ella?"

I held up my hand for her to remain quiet while my mind juggled all the pieces and eventually morphed them into a picture I could see.

"Oh, my goodness!" I dashed back to the telephone and called Baxter again.

"I didn't think I'd hear from you quite so soon, Miss Bridges."

"Baxter, can you come to Claridges urgently? I've just discovered something important. We're in suite 212."

From the tone of my voice he knew not to waste time asking questions. "I'm on my way."

Back in the living room Aunt Margaret had the pills and a glass of water for me. I swallowed them down quickly, then asked her to telephone Bunny. He needed to come immediately. She did so, then returned asking what it was all about.

"I've discovered something important, Aunt Margaret, but I'll go through it when everyone's here rather than repeat myself if that's alright with you?"

"Of course it is, dear."

Twenty minutes after I had called him the second time, Baxter was announced by our butler. A few minutes later Bunny arrived too. The two men shook hands and Aunt Margaret and I greeted them both warmly. Baxter looked tired and worn, which worried me, and I made a mental note to have a proper talk with him once the case was over and get to the bottom of his troubles.

"Snow said it was urgent on the telephone, Miss Bridges, what have you discovered?" asked Bunny.

"The day we first met I told you I was working on the murder of Josephine Brown. You seemed shocked at the news."

"What? Of course I was shocked. What sort of question is that?"

"Please, just bear with me. We now know she was one of your agents, but who was her handler?"

"Vera White. Why?"

"Has she been with you long?"

"Years. She's a good agent and handles several agents of her own. Look, what is all this about?"

"Can you describe her for me?"

Bunny narrowed his eyes. "I hope you have a good reason for this, Miss Bridges."

"I do."

"Alright. She's fifty four, plain looking and a bit on the plump side and..."

"With an unsightly mole on her chin," I finished for him.

"Yes. How on earth would you know that?"

I glanced at Baxter who nodded in understanding. "The Dame," he said to me.

"Yes."

"Dame. What dame? What are you talking about?"

"Just hear me out, Bunny. It will all make sense in a moment. On hearing the news of Miss Brown's death, if you remember, you made the decision not to tell the rest of the staff for morale's sake. Did you abide by that decision?"

"I did."

"Including Vera White? You didn't tell her either?"

"I did not."

"What did you tell her?"

"That Miss Brown was taking a short holiday and that she, Vera, was needed elsewhere. I gave her another job to do. She still doesn't know about Josephine Brown's murder."

"I'm afraid she does, Bunny. She's known from almost the beginning because Baxter and I told her."

"What?" he glanced at Baxter then back at me. "What do you mean you told her?"

I nodded to Baxter to take up the reins. It had been he who'd discovered the dame in the first place so this part of the story was his to convey. I also wanted him to feel part of the investigation again. He cleared his throat.

"As you are aware, once Miss Bridges and I had discovered the identity of Miss Brown, it naturally led us to her employers, the Parfitts. As part of the enquiry we interviewed them and I asked whether they had obtained references for the nanny. Elizabeth Parfitt gave us the name of her previous employer, one Dame Mildred Pocklington. I tracked down Dame Pocklington and Miss Bridges and I interviewed her at Lyons Corner House in The Strand. Obviously, we told her that Miss Brown had been murdered. The person you've just described as your agent Vera White is the same woman who disguised herself as Dame Pocklington."

"Well, there's a perfectly good explanation for that," Bunny said. "In order to keep secret the real identity of our agents we have to put in place some considerable history for them. A back story if you like. Vera was just protecting her agent."

Bunny's interpretation was more than feasible, but I wasn't convinced Vera White was as pure or virtuous as her name would suggest.

"I'm sorry, Bunny. I just have a few more questions. Going back to the day when I first met you and broke the news of Josephine's death, can you remember if Vera was in your offices sometime before Aunt Margaret and I arrived?"

Bunny looked up, his eyes filled with misery as he tried to remember. Eventually he nodded. "Yes, yes she was. She left perhaps three quarters of an hour before you arrived."

"And she didn't tell you about Josephine's murder?"

"You know she didn't. How do you know she'd been there?"

"Because I saw her coming out of the Tailor's on Jermyn Street when we arrived. Aunt Margaret and I were waiting across the road. I had every intention of following her but she hopped on a bus so I couldn't. With the surprise of everything that followed, the use of the nonsensical code phrase that worked in Noble and Vaughn's, the travel down a secret tunnel under London and the discovery of the Secret Intelligence Service in the bowels of the city, I completely forgot about her."

"I did too," said my aunt.

"Unfortunately, the fact remains that one of your senior people knew about the murder of a SIS agent undercover, one she handled, yet she didn't report it to you. Surely that would have been her first course of action? Mandatory I would think?" Bunny nodded in reply.

"I should have remembered it sooner and for that I am sorry, Bunny. But I'm afraid Vera White must be considered hostile. She's quite obviously a double agent."

———◆———

"OH, DEAR GOD," HE SAID softly, looking at my aunt in horror. His face had turned the colour of waxed paper.

"I'll get you a drink, Bunny," she said, rising. "Then you must contact Carstairs to apprehend Vera White immediately."

Bunny gulped down his brandy in one go. Then stood up to use the telephone. My Aunt followed, and I heard her saying how sorry she was it had come to this.

"I've had a good innings, Snow. Let's make sure we get them, shall we?" he replied as they drifted out of hearing.

"Well done, Miss Bridges."

"Thank you, Baxter, although I don't feel particularly happy about it. I feel quite dreadful for Bunny."

"Do you think this Vera White had something to do with Miss Brown's Murder?"

"I wouldn't be surprised. It certainly explains why nothing was found to implicate Parfitt earlier. Josephine Brown was passing on any findings to a double agent. This case has been filled with people leading double lives from the outset, my aunt and I included to some extent. Thank goodness I can rely on you, Baxter. I don't know what I'd do if you disappeared."

"Well, about that, Miss Bridges…"

But I never heard what he was about to say as Bunny and Aunt Margaret returned.

"Bunny has contacted Carstairs and they're now actively searching for Vera White. He'll telephone here when he has news. It's now more important than ever that we break this latest code, Ella."

"I realise that, Aunt Margaret, but I'm not sure how to start?"

"Sorry for interrupting," Baxter said. "But I was of the understanding you needed some of my men to keep watch at the airports. Is that still the case?"

Bunny shook his head. "It's appreciated, Baxter, but in light of what we've just found out we'll have to assume they know our next steps. We'll hold off on that for now, but I may need you later depending on what the ladies find?"

"I'm at your disposal. Just telephone me at the yard if you need me."

Baxter said his goodbyes and shortly after Bunny left too. He had a monumental crisis to deal with.

"How sadly ironic the mole has a mole," my aunt said.

I smiled at the attempt to lighten the despondent mood. As jokes went it was rather a good one, but my heart wasn't really in it.

"What did Bunny mean when he said, 'I've had a good innings?'" I asked her.

"There's been a double agent working in the very heart of the Secret Intelligence Service, Ella. For years. Heads will roll for this and I'm afraid Bunny's will be the first on the block. He knows it too."

"But that's hardly fair. How was he supposed to know? No one else had worked it out either."

"No, but he's in charge of the department and Vera White was a key member of the agency, a team leader handling agents of her own. It was Bunny who promoted her to that position. As unfair as it sounds someone has to take the blame."

"So, he's the scapegoat then?"

"Bunny will take the blame himself and willingly. I expect he'll tender his resignation once this case is over. He's a good man, Ella, one of the best in fact, but he made a grave error of judgment. He knows he did and will take the fall. It's a distressing end to what has otherwise been a glittering career, but there really is no other way. His card is marked."

"Then let us make sure we solve this case and catch the spies, Aunt Margaret. It's the least we can do for him."

"We don't have long, Ella. The letter should have gone in the post on Friday evening, so would have been delivered today. Considering it said forty-eight hours to the extraction, Arnister and Batholomew will be leaving the country at some point late tomorrow night or the early hours of Monday morning."

"We need to find the code-phrase. But where do we start?"

"I'll order some coffee. We're going to need it."

———◉———

"I FELT SURE THIS WOULD be it, Aunt Margaret. What are we going to do?"

"We can't give up, Ella, there's too much at stake."

"But there's nothing left in the book to work from."

"Wait, that's the telephone."

I threw the book on the table in disgust, cursing Richard Hannay and the world in general, and went to pour myself a stiff drink while Aunt Margaret answered the call. Surely the whole case couldn't end like this? We were so close! Suddenly there was a crash, and I turned to see three of the five ceramic pigs had fallen from the mantelpiece and smashed in the hearth.

Aunt Margaret came rushing in, having finished her call, "Ella, what happened?" she said as she stared at the mess in dismay.

"Phantom," I said, making a move to clear up the damage. "Who was on the telephone?"

"Carstairs asking for updates. Bunny is out searching for Vera White. I told him I'd call when we knew something. Look, just leave that, darling, we have more important things to do. Let's go back through the book, there must be something in there that will help us. Are you sure we've been though everything that Nightingale wrote herself?"

"Yes. The only thing left is the list of nursery rhymes." I paused. "I don't believe it." I said as I stared at the carnage in the hearth.

I rushed back to the book and opened the very first page. There in Josephine Brown's own hand writing was a list of twelve well known nursery rhymes.

"Well, is it there?"

"Yes, third on the list. Three Little Pigs."

My heart began to thump as Aunt Margaret set to, trying to fit the title into the grid. We were close, I could feel it.

"That doesn't work either. What could it possibly be?"

"Probably too literal, but let me check chapter three."

I swiftly turned to the correct page. "Oh, good heavens, it mentions ciphers, Aunt Margaret! The chapter title is, 'The Adventure of the Literary Inn-keeper.'"

More scribbling and mumbling from my aunt as she worked it through but again it just didn't work.

"What's the first letter of chapter three?" she demanded.

"*I*"

I held my breath and watched over her shoulder as she inserted the alphabet into the grid starting at the letter I. Suddenly four letters were revealed, the most we'd had previously was one. My aunt looked up at me, eyes shining.

"We've got it, Ella!"

She hurriedly completed the rest of the code.

"Quickly! What does it say?"

Heston Airfield. One am. Sunday 25th.

"What? They know we're onto them! They've brought the extraction forward! Aunt Margaret, that's-" I glanced at the clock. "Just under three hours away. We'll never make it!"

Chapter Sixteen

"ELLA, CALL BAXTER. Tell him to pick us up immediately and to bring as many plain-clothes men as he can spare. Destination Heston airfield."

I ran to the phone and dialled Scotland Yard only to be told Baxter had gone home. Of course he had, it was ridiculously late, he wouldn't still be working. Luckily due to his position he had a telephone installed. I glanced at my watch, just after a quarter past ten, I hoped he hadn't retired for the night.

A sleepy male voice answered.

"Baxter? It's Ella, sorry if I woke you but we've broken the code. The plan has changed. They're leaving tonight from Heston Aerodrome. Can you come and pick us up from Claridges and bring as many plain clothes chaps as possible?"

"I'll be there as soon as I can. Is there anything else you need?"

I asked him for one more thing, said goodbye and called out to my aunt.

"In here, Ella."

I ran to her bedroom to find she'd changed into a working man's outfit. Dark slacks, jacket and boots and a black neckerchief. She'd also laid out a similar ensemble for me. Including a dark poacher's coat. That would work perfectly for what I'd asked Baxter to bring me.

Aunt Margaret took a small gun from her nightstand and, checking it was fully loaded, slipped it into her pocket.

"Gosh, I hope it won't come to that," I said.

"You're not the only one, Ella, but we need to be prepared for the worst. Now, hurry up and get changed while I telephone Carstairs. I assume Baxter is coming?"

"Yes, he'll be about half an hour, I should think. He was arranging for additional men after we'd spoken."

"Jolly good. There's a flat cap there for you and a belt."

I was fully attired and just stuffing my hair inside the cap when she returned.

"Right, Carstairs is scrambling the troops. Still no contact from Bunny but he has someone looking for him."

"I assume they still have men watching Arnister and Batholomew?"

"Yes, and they'll keep doing so. No doubt they'll follow them to Heston."

"Where is the Aerodrome exactly?"

"Hounslow."

"But that's miles away!"

"Twelve, give or take."

"We really are cutting this fine, Aunt Margaret, It's almost eleven o'clock now."

"Better get a move on then, hadn't we, dear?"

We rode the lift to the ground floor in silence, the operator politely ignoring our bizarre clothing and wishing us a good evening as we departed. The doorman outside did the same, tipping his hat and asking if we'd like a taxi which we declined. Goodness knows what they were actually thinking seeing two well-to-do women dressed as working men. Their reputation of discretion had certainly been put to the test, and they had passed with flying colours.

Twenty minutes later Baxter pulled up in a black Wolseley and we hastened into the back. Riding as a passenger was a plain-clothed officer I hadn't met before, and Baxter assured us there were more already on the way to the airfield.

"They'll meet us at a secure spot just outside," he informed us, pulling away from the kerb. "So what's the plan?"

I looked at Aunt Margaret questioningly. I hadn't thought that far ahead.

"Get to the airfield, stop the plane, arrest the spies and try not to get hurt," she said. Obviously she hadn't thought much further either.

———— ◉ ————

IT WAS CLOSE TO MIDNIGHT when we arrived on the outskirts of Heston Aerodrome and the tension was palpable. We had no more than an hour to catch Arnister, Batholomew and whomever else they were with, before they took off and we lost them forever.

Baxter parked amidst the cover of a stand of trees to the South next to the two other cars containing eight of his best officers.

"Does anyone know the layout of the airfield?" my aunt asked. "It would be better not to go in blind if we can."

"I do, Ma'am," the passenger of our car replied and brought forth a hurriedly scribbled map. I had noticed he was busy sketching by the light of a torch during the journey. He spread it out on the bonnet of the car and Baxter called everyone round.

The entrance to the site was signposted by two large white posts and the road carried straight on until it reached a turning circle at the front entrance.

The main buildings were two-storey with the tower on top of the central one. To the left and right were other adjoining buildings, which I assumed consisted of waiting and luggage areas. And further out still on both sides, but on the main West to East trajectory, were large hangars for the aircraft. At the other side of the row of buildings it was predominately grassed for the takeoff and landing of the planes and beyond that was suburban housing for the areas of Heston and Cranford.

"Right," said Baxter. "I think we split into two teams and use a pincer movement coming in from both sides. There's wire fencing surrounding the site but we have the necessary tools to get through those. We'll worry about the consequences later."

"My type of plan, Baxter," Aunt Margaret said. "Are there guards, do you know?"

"Some guards patrolling the perimeter, Ma'am," the map-maker said. "But not many. We should be able to get through the fence with little trouble. It'll be the dash across the open area that'll be the problem. Lit up like a Christmas tree when aircraft are due. Although it looks strangely quiet at the moment."

"Yes. I doubt there'll be other flights tonight, our spies won't want any interference," my aunt agreed. "Well, I'm afraid there's nothing else for it. We'll just have to run like the wind and hope we're not seen."

Baxter then designated the teams. Aunt Margaret, myself, the mapmaker, and two others would join Baxter and go in from the West Side, the other six would head in from the East.

When the other team had set off to their start position, Baxter handed me what I'd asked for. It was a truncheon and it fit perfectly in the long, left-hand pocket inside my poacher's coat.

"Thank you, Baxter. I feel much better with some sort of weapon."

"I see you're already set up," Baxter said, eyeing my aunt's gun.

"Don't worry, Baxter, I have a license for it and plenty of experience."

"I don't doubt it for a moment," he said, then paused and looked at us both in turn. "Before we go in, I'd just like to say that I'm not at all happy about you two risking your lives like this. But..." he held up a hand knowing we'd disagree. "I know the two of you well enough to realise you won't be put off by something as trifling as my concern. Just be careful."

"Oh, Baxter, you are a dear," I said. "And your concern is hardly trifling. We appreciate it, don't we, Aunt Margaret?"

"We do indeed. And by the same token you be careful too. These are dangerous people under normal circumstances, let alone when cornered and threatened. Just make sure you don't put yourself at risk by trying to protect Ella or myself. We can manage perfectly well on our own."

And on that rather ominous note we headed off to break through a fence.

<hr>

WE'D JUST GOT INTO position, crouched behind the perimeter wire with one of Baxter's men making an opening with bolt cutters, when I spied the headlights of a vehicle coming up the main road to the airfield buildings.

"Look!" I said. "Is that them? I can't see from this distance."

Baxter took a pair of field glasses from his pocket and handed them to me.

"Have a look and tell us, Miss Bridges. I'd recognise the woman, but not the other two."

I brought the glasses to my eyes and after a moment of fiddling with the focus, I found my quarry.

"It is them. Vera White driving, Batholomew in the passenger side and I assume it's Arnister in the rear. They're stopping in front of the main building."

I handed the glasses to Baxter who took a look, then handed them to Aunt Margaret, who in turn passed them on. We now all knew who we were looking for. The other team would have to work on the assumption that the passengers for the only flight out this night were the ones we wanted to apprehend.

The bolt cutters made short work of the fence and one by one we scrambled through. Keeping low, we ran in a crouched line format, the nearside hangar our destination, when halfway across someone called out in a loud whisper.

"Lights! Get down."

Without a second thought, all six of us fell flat to the ground, arms over our heads to cover pale faces and waited for the lights to sweep across. It seemed an absolute age lying on the cold damp earth. My heart was racing and all I could hear was the rushing of blood in my ears. I saw the light swing over in an arc trained on the outer fence, then swing back. As it passed back and forth it got nearer and nearer and nearer. I held my breath, peeking out from under my arm as it got closer. This could be it, one more sweep and we'd be caught!

I heard my aunt whisper, 'For heaven's sake!' Then the light swept away and went out. leaving us once more in darkness. I let out a shaky relieved breath. It had missed us only by a few feet. If we'd stopped any further back, we'd have been spotted.

"All clear," said the same voice. One of Baxter's men whom I didn't know.

"That was a bit too close," I whispered.

We scrambled back to our crouching positions and ran pell-mell across the expanse of ground, coming to rest a few minutes later against the large side of the hangar.

We sunk down onto our haunches, backs against the wall while we caught our breath.

"I'm going to have a look at the front," I whispered to Baxter, who nodded.

Still doubled over I crept forward to the end of the hangar and peered around the corner. The front was a wide strip of concrete which abutted the grassed area. Lined up in front of the three adjacent hangars were several airplanes, but which one would the traitors use? I worked my way down the line and realised that all, bar the one at the far end were two-seaters. The largest had three side windows which meant a minimum of six passengers. This was definitely the plane the spies were planning to escape in.

I was about to retreat from my reconnoitre when I saw a pilot exit the farthest hangar followed by a second man in similar uniform. The co-pilot I assumed. They were heading to the larger plane. There wasn't a moment to lose.

I scurried back to my waiting colleagues and told them what I'd observed.

"We can't go across the front, we'll be seen," I hissed. "Is there a way at the back of these hangars? We need to get nearer."

"Stubbs?" asked Baxter.

It was the mapmaker who answered.

"The hangars are all built separately, so there's a ginnel between each one. We should be able to get access around the back."

"Right, come on then. Be quiet and remain alert."

In single file, with Stubbs leading the way and me bringing up the rear, we crept to the end of the hangar. Stubbs held up his hand for us to stop and stuck his head round the bend. After a moment he motioned for us to continue and we slinked around the corner like a snake, keeping to the shadows the wall cast.

Used as it was to house several planes side by side, the hangar was enormous and it took us a while to get to the foremost passage running between the first and second buildings. One at a time we ran across the opening gap making sure we weren't seen from the other end, then continued down the back of the second building. This one was even larger than the first and I was beginning to panic that we'd run out of time. If the plane began to taxi around to the beginning of the runway with the passengers aboard, there would be no way on earth we could stop it.

I tapped the shoulder of the man in front and whispered to him, "Pass it on. We need to move a bit faster, we've got less than half an hour!"

A moment later we were trotting at a better speed and almost at the start of the next passage. Once again Stubbs held up his hand for us to stop, but this time flapped it downward, meaning crouch down. We all did so, then we heard the sound of voices coming from the end of the narrow alley where the airplanes were.

The language was foreign, Russian I assumed, but there was no mistaking the supercilious tones of Edward Batholomew.

Stubbs turned. "They're right at the end of the ginnel. I'm not sure we can cross without being seen, although there's a few packing crates stacked up at one side which might give us some cover."

"What about some sort of diversion?" I suggested.

"Let's not give ourselves away before we need to," Baxter said.

"I could always shoot them," Aunt Margaret added.

"You're surrounded by The Yard's finest," I said. "I doubt you'd get away with it."

"Does anyone know what they're saying?" asked Baxter, keeping a sensible rein on things.

Aunt Margaret crept in front of Stubbs and listened carefully.

"My Russian is a little rusty I'm afraid, but mostly they can't wait to leave. Some joke or other about pulling the wool over our eyes. Well really! And... Ah, there appears to be a bit of a delay for some reason. One of their party is missing, I think. Well, that's good news for us. Wait, they're leaving. Coffee awaits apparently. We should be able to cross now."

Stubbs checked they'd gone, then indicated we could move.

"Hang about," I said. "Shouldn't we advance from both sides? You know, a pincer movement?"

Baxter turned to me. "Yes, that's probably a better idea, actually. How would you prefer to do it, Miss Bridges?"

"Aunt Margaret, you go with Stubbs and... I'm sorry, I don't know your names?"

"Apologies. This is Peak and Walker," Baxter said.

"Right. Aunt Margaret, Stubbs and Peak, you carry on to the other side of the hangar, then turn down the side and follow it to where the aircraft is. Sergeant Baxter, myself and Walker will wait until you're at the other end and then advance slowly down this passage way. If all goes to plan, we'll meet you at the front and take captive our spies."

With that organised the other three, led by my aunt, dashed across the gap and continued up the back of the final hangar. We watched them, Peak slowing down a little while the other two raced on ahead. Peak was a good few yards behind them when the unthinkable happened. A door in the back of the hangar opened. Peak smashed into it and crumpled to the floor. We were exposed!

<hr />

"QUICK! INTO THE PASSAGE," I said.

We dived for the entrance and hid just as a shout went up from the man who'd opened the door. On all fours, I stuck my head back round the corner and saw Peak was knocked out cold. I hoped Aunt Margaret and Stubbs were alright. Luckily the open door had blocked the view of them.

"Peak's not got identification on him, has he?" I whispered to Baxter.

"No. Although he'll be carrying a police truncheon. Let's hope they don't recognise it as such."

"And let's hope Peak doesn't come round for a while. They'll definitely know he's an intruder. As long as he can't answer any questions, we should still have the element of surprise. But we need to move. Quickly! To the other end of this passage."

We scrambled as best we could up the side of the hangar. I was leading, with Baxter next and Walker at the end. It was difficult going. Trying to be fast and quiet was hard work, not to mention being doubled over for so long was causing my neck and back to ache dreadfully.

A few feet before the end where the passage opened to the expanse of concrete at the front, I stopped and straightened up. I took a moment to stretch my back and roll my neck to ease out the kinks, then edged my way forward. With a quick glimpse round the corner to get the lay of the land I darted back.

"Batholomew and Arnister have just headed inside the hangar," I whispered to Baxter. "No doubt to see what all the fuss is about. I expect they're bringing Peak in."

We could hear raised voices coming from inside toward the back of the building.

"I don't know how many are in there but we need to get inside."

Baxter nodded once then with another quick look to check the coast was clear, I scampered round the corner. The doors were a concertinaed design and opened all the way on both sides. I ran a couple of steps and nipped into the hangar.

I had expected it to be almost empty with space for the aircraft, but this was obviously a storage and maintenance hangar. It was row upon row of twenty-foot high shelving packed with large machine parts, tools, boxes and other things I didn't recognise. I'm sure it was configured in a logical way, but to me it looked like a maze. Although it certainly helped to conceal me. It smelled of oil and paraffin overlaid with dust and paint. It was also dark, the only lights coming from the strip at the centre of the hangar, the periphery left to blackness and shadow.

I ducked down behind the nearest shelf and slowly edged my way forward. At the end I took a left, quietly working my way toward the middle of the building and the voices.

I'd not gone far when I suddenly realised neither Baxter nor Walker had followed me. I was on my own! I took a deep breath and wiped clammy hands down my coat. I could do this. No doubt Aunt Margaret was at the other side mirroring my movements. I hoped so at least.

I was halfway down the next stack of shelving when a man's voice called out.

"Wait, I think I heard something?"

Then horror. Footsteps coming closer. Where could I hide? I frantically looked around and suddenly spied a gap on a bottom shelf. Quickly I crawled in and crouched behind a wooden box, trying not to breathe.

The footsteps got closer, followed by the beam of a torch as it scanned the walk space between the shelving.

"Anything?" another voice called out from further away.

"No. Must have been a rat."

A rat? I swallowed the scream that burbled in my throat as the footsteps and the torch retreated. After a few seconds of deep breathing to calm my hammering pulse, I slowly crawled out and began to move.

I tiptoed carefully, taking a right turn at another intersection while gradually edging forward and peering between the shelves. My quarry was now in sight.

Suddenly I was wrenched backward. An arm tightened around my neck and a blade pressed savagely against my throat.

Chapter Seventeen

IN MY SHORT CAREER as a detective I'd only been truly frightened twice. As the sharp blade sliced my skin and a drop of blood trickled down my neck, that number increased to three. I gulped as tears sprang to my eyes. My career had been short but my life was about to be shorter.

"One word and you're dead," a voice whispered in my ear.

Vera White! I recognised it at once. I'd been so caught up in the threat of Arnister and Batholomew, I'd seriously underestimated the woman. A mistake that could cost me my life.

"Your pathetic attempts will not stop our plans, Miss Bridges. You've been lucky so far, but luck has to run out sometime."

"You killed Nightingale," I whispered, conscious of the knife.

"She got too close. Just as you have."

A vague shimmering at the end of a shelf caught my eye and Phantom appeared. Without moving my head, I glanced to the bottom of the shelf, and just peeking out round the corner was the toe of a boot. I nearly cried out with relief at the knowledge I wasn't alone. But how could they help me in this predicament?

Then suddenly I was struck by a flash of inspiration. I had no idea if it would work. But it was my only chance.

I bent my knees feigning a swoon. The grip on my neck loosened. A shot rang out, and the knife dropped. Vera staggered back and in one fluid motion I reached into my left inside pocket, grabbed my cosh, pivoted on one foot and hit her across the temple. She dropped like a sack of potatoes. Not a sound passed from her lips.

"Good reflexes, Ella."

"Good shot, Aunt Margaret."

Suddenly there was a loud commotion from outside. Yells and screams followed by pounding feet across concrete and several gun shots echoed around the hangar.

"Quickly, tie her up."

I checked Vera's pulse and found she was alive. I undid my belt and tied her feet. Aunt Margaret did the same with her hands. Then we gagged her with our neckerchiefs and dragged her to the side of the building out of the way.

We scurried back to the centre of the hangar and ducked behind a shelf. I could see Peak still out cold on the floor near the closed rear door and wondered if he was alright. Arnister and Batholomew were hiding behind an upturned desk, returning fire to several armed men at the entrance to the building. The Secret Intelligence Service had arrived!

"What can we do from here?" I asked.

"Wait."

"Don't worry, I'm not charging into the affray armed with only a billy club. Which reminds me, when this is all over I want you to teach me how to shoot."

"Are you sure, dear?" she said calmly, as though we were having tea instead of being in the middle of a battle-field.

I ducked as a stray bullet ricocheted off a metal joist and went whizzing past my ear.

"It's either that or I become an English teacher. Which is beginning to sound more and more attractive. I really think we should move to somewhere safer."

We scuttled back a couple of yards, still not safe enough to my mind but Aunt Margaret insisted. We still had a view of the spies returning the SIS volley and the back door.

"What are we waiting for?"

"That," she said, pointing to the rear exit which was just beginning to open.

<hr />

I HELD MY BREATH AND watched as the door opened a fraction and the head of Carstairs flashed in momentarily, then vanished. A second later the door was pulled open and Carstairs reappeared. Hunched low he fired two shots while simultaneously rolling across the floor, ending in a crouched position safely behind the nearest shelf.

His marksmanship was utterly superb. He'd caught Arnister in the wrist and Batholomew in the shoulder. Both men yelled and dropped their guns. Carstairs yelled out, "Clear! Carstairs!" for the benefit of the SIS men at the door who after a moment stopped firing. Then Baxter and Walker emerged, rushing to the two spies, throwing them face down and cuffing them.

Aunt Margaret and I surged across to Peak to check on his vitals. His pulse was fine and as I began to slap his cheek his eyelids fluttered. Aunt Margaret held some smelling salts under his nose and he came to rapidly then. His hand went to the back of his head where he'd hit the ground and came away slick with blood. His forehead had a nice egg-shaped bump on it too.

"Bloody hell! What happened?"

"You hit a door at speed, my good man. Then followed it up with the ground. What's your name?" Aunt Margaret asked.

"Peak, Sergeant."

"And how many fingers am I holding up, Sergeant Peak?"

"Three."

"Correct. You're alright, although you may need a couple of stitches and I'm afraid you'll have a humdinger of a headache for a while."

"It'll make a change from the wife, I suppose," Peak replied drolly.

As my aunt administered aid to Peak, I went in search of Baxter. I found him outside with Walker, handing over Arnister and Batholomew to Bunny.

"Well done, Baxter!" I said. Then I turned to Bunny, "You'll find Vera White tied up at the far side of the hangar. She has a bullet in her shoulder and I had to crack her across the head, but she's breathing."

"Excellent job, Miss Bridges. Is Snow alright?"

"Yes, she's fine. Administering first aid to Peak presently, and sharing ribald jokes from what I could hear. But she'll be along shortly. Oh, one other thing. Vera confessed to killing Josephine Brown."

He clenched his jaw, nodded once, then left to organise the retrieval of Vera. I think he was rather looking forward to it.

"Your neck is bleeding, Miss Bridges."

I gingerly touched where Vera had held the knife and my fingers came away slightly sticky.

"Courtesy of Vera White. Don't worry, Baxter, it's superficial and has almost stopped now. So, where did you and Walker disappear to? I thought you were behind me when I dashed into the hangar?"

"We were about to but just as you'd entered the two pilots appeared, heading our way. We couldn't let an opportunity like that pass us by so we waited until they were just at the entrance, then jumped them both. They didn't stand a chance. Walker and me had them trussed up before they could say boo to a goose. Then the SIS arrived, and it turned into a gun battle. Carstairs came up behind us and told us his plan to come in from the rear and take Arnister and Batholomew by surprise. We teamed up with him and the rest you know."

"The perfect pincer movement, Baxter."

"It was indeed, Miss Bridges. It was indeed."

Chapter Eighteen

THE DAYS FOLLOWING the successful capture of Arnister, Batholomew, White and the two pilots were spent in a plethora of meetings and interviews. Some as an observer, utilising my skills, and others as an interviewee recounting my actions and the part I had played in the operation. It was paramount a comprehensive picture was formed and an extensive report written, so that such a catastrophic failure of our country's security would never be repeated. The report once completed would remain Top Secret, accessible to only a few at the highest level. Mistakes would be pored over, dissected and used to improve intelligence training going forward.

Prime Minister Baldwin was continuing the daily business of running the country in the public eye, but late into the night he was ensconced in meetings with top level cabinet ministers and on several occasions the King himself.

The fact that four double agents had been discovered working in such strategic positions had rocked the establishment to its core. The significant threat to the Empire couldn't be underestimated and behind closed doors various Government Ministers were demanding an internal inquiry. Heads would roll. The first, as Aunt Margaret had warned me, was Bunny's.

I scoured the newspapers daily for articles pertaining to the breach and news of the capture of the Russian spies, but there was nothing. As Bunny had informed Parfitt during the interview at the safe house in Nassau Street, the Government would do everything in its power to keep the truth from becoming public knowledge. It looked as though they'd succeeded.

It was on a Sunday, a week later, that Aunt Margaret and I, now finished with the official inquiry, found ourselves walking through Kensington Palace Gardens.

"This is where it all began," I said, as we approached the statue of Peter Pan. "So much has happened since. It's quite surreal."

She smiled and linked her arm through mine as we meandered along the footpath adjacent to The Long Water, heading toward the Italian Gardens.

"Have you decided what you're wearing to the palace, Ella?"

That had been another quite surreal moment. Apparently, Aunt Margaret, Baxter and I were all to be presented with medals of honour for services to King and Country. The ceremony would take place at Buckingham Palace four days hence with the King himself presenting the medals. Of course, it was all to be done under the strictest secrecy. No one would ever know and we would never be able to talk about it. But it was a great honour, nonetheless.

"I confess I haven't really given it much thought," I said.

"Worrying about Baxter still?"

"Yes, but I've made arrangements to meet him for lunch tomorrow and I shall refuse to leave until he tells me what the problem is."

"Do you think he will?"

"I believe he was just to about to the other day, actually. It was when the four of us were meeting in our suite, and you and Bunny had just returned from telephoning Carstairs about apprehending Vera White. The moment was lost after that and we haven't found the time since. But I do think he'll tell me, yes. I just hope I can help solve the problem."

We continued to walk around the Italian Garden fountains, passed Queen Anne's Alcove and continued our way down North Carriage Drive. At Speakers Corner we joined Cumberland Gate and left the park to walk down Bayswater Road, heading towards Marble Arch.

"So, what will happen to Bunny now, Aunt Margaret? I feel simply dreadful that the poor man has lost his job."

"Don't take it to heart so, dear. It's true he has retired, but it was at his own instigation."

"Before they pushed him out, you mean."

"Not necessarily. I think he would have been sidelined as opposed to let go completely, which wouldn't have suited him at all. But this way he has control of his future and can pick and choose. His people are in Kent somewhere so I suspect he'll stay there for a while, contemplating his options. He's a clever man, Ella, with a set of skills and experiences which are unique. I doubt it will be the last we hear of dear old Bunny."

"You know something. don't you?"

She laughed. "Well, of course I do. But I can't say any more. Now, it appears we've walked all the way to Mayfair, dear."

I looked around and found she was right, but my surroundings were very familiar. I looked at the town house across the road and found it in darkness, the curtains drawn across the windows and an estate agent board attached to the iron railing.

"It's for sale."

"So it is. Well now, this is interesting. The perfect neighbourhood. What do you think? Shall I buy it?"

"It's the Parfitt's old house, Aunt Margaret."

"Is it really? All the better then."

"You wouldn't mind? knowing it had belonged to a traitor?"

"Not in the slightest. It's only bricks and mortar. Besides, we're all spies, aren't we? This way it will at least belong to someone on the right side for a change."

"Then you'd better make a note of the telephone number. We can call when we get back to Claridges."

Just before we turned to retrace our route home, Phantom appeared outside the garden gate, then seconds later Josephine Brown materialised next to him. She gave me a small smile and a nod, then the two of them walked away, slowly fading until they vanished completely.

My job here was finished.

AT TWELVE FORTY-FIVE on Monday, I met Baxter outside Simpson's in The Strand where we had arranged to have lunch. It was one of London's oldest traditional English restaurants, famous for its roasts, having had a modest start as a smoking room in 1828 then shortly after, a coffee house. Its keynote being solid comfort, the author P. G. Wodehouse had called it 'a restful temple of food,' and I wholeheartedly agreed with him. There was little in the way of distractions and we would be assured of a private corner for the conversation I had planned. I hoped to entice Baxter to share what was troubling him.

"Good afternoon, Miss Bridges."

"Hello, Baxter. How are you?"

"Can't complain. And you?"

"Much the same. Shall we go in?"

The maître d' asked if we had a reservation and Baxter informed him we had, under the name Bridges.

"Of course, sir. I have been asked to tell you that the cost of your dining today has all been taken care of."

"Taken care of?" I asked. I looked at Baxter in puzzlement but he shrugged and shook his head. I turned back to the maître d', "Do you know who by?"

"I was told to give you this if you asked, Miss."

He handed me a small envelope from which I pulled forth a postcard with the image of a white rabbit on the front. There was no handwriting but Baxter and I knew at once who it was from and shared a smile.

"Thank you," I said, putting the card in my handbag. "We're ready to go through now."

We were shown to a table at the far end of The Grand Divan dining room next to the window where our conversation wouldn't be overheard.

Over the first course of soup and freshly baked crusty rolls, we spoke about the case and the exhausting round of interviews and meetings we'd been subject to in recent days. The fact that we were to be honoured at the palace and the distinct lack of reporting in the newspapers pertaining to the inquiry as a whole.

Over the main roast course, expertly cut and served by the chef at our table, I decided to turn to the matter at hand. I was thinking of a suitably tactful way to begin when Baxter did it for me.

"I'm aware of the reason you suggested lunch, Miss Bridges."

"You are? Oh, thank goodness. I've been wracking my brains as to how to politely broach the subject. So, what has been troubling you? I don't mind admitting I have been awfully concerned. You're not just my colleague you know, Baxter, you're my friend and I'd like to help if I can."

He laid down his cutlery and wiped his mouth with the napkin before taking a deep breath.

"It's Mrs Baxter. She wants us to leave London and move to the coast. Devon or Cornwall or somewhere like that. Near the seaside, she says. She's completely sick of London."

I was struck dumb for a minute or two while the import of his words struck home.

"But that will mean you'd have to leave The Yard!"

"Yes, it looks that way."

"Oh, Baxter, I'm so dreadfully sorry. I take it Mrs Baxter's mind is made up?"

"I'm afraid so, Miss Bridges. But the important thing is I can't abide seeing my wife so unhappy. If it means I have to join a smaller police station, then I'll do so. I'll still have a job and Mrs Baxter will be all the more happy for it. She's put up with me for all these years, it's the least I can do."

"You're such a good man, you know. Mrs Baxter is very lucky to have you."

"It's more the other way round, Miss Bridges, but thank you for saying so."

We made further small talk and over coffee I asked if he'd enjoyed his lunch.

"It was very good indeed. Not quite as good as my wife's, of course, but very close."

"Oh, yes I remember you saying she was an excellent cook..." and then it suddenly came to me.

"Oh, Baxter! I do believe I have the perfect solution to your problem."

———◉———

"DO YOU NOW? I'D LIKE to hear what you have in mind, Miss Bridges."

"Remember when I telephoned my housekeeper to ask if the storm had done any damage to my home?"

"Yes. You said there wasn't much, luckily."

"I did. But the Suntrap School didn't come off quite so well. One of their classrooms, a rather rickety wooden building unfortunately, collapsed completely. My gardener Tom is helping to rebuild it."

"I don't think I've heard of the school."

"It's a special place for children from the inner city areas, dirt poor in the main and in general ill health. Respiratory problems mostly due to the air quality and cramped living conditions. Some physical and mental issues, but not many. They're taught all the basic subjects and benefit greatly from the sunshine and sea air, as you can imagine. It's a wonderful place for them."

"I'm with you so far, but don't quite see how it's relevant."

"Well, my housekeeper informed me that after the storm one of the teachers stumbled on the debris and broke her leg. She's decided to retire finally and move in with her sister in Wales. They're looking for a replacement. Guess what she used to teach, Baxter."

"Er, well now. I'm not sure. English perhaps?"

"No, Baxter," I laughed. "She used to teach cookery. They need someone to instruct these children to cook and bake and do housekeeping. Don't you think this would be the perfect job for Mrs Baxter? It's within walking distance of the beach as well. And what's more I know of a perfect home for rent just off the main street too. Two bedrooms and a garden front and rear. It would be perfect and you'd not have to leave The Yard as you'd only be an hour away on the train, like me. So, what do you think? Would Mrs Baxter be open to the idea?"

"Do you know, Miss Bridges, I think she might very well be. She does like Linhay Island very much. I shall have a word with her this evening."

And that's exactly what he did.

A week later he telephoned me at Gerry and Ginny's. Aunt Margaret and I were staying with them again before I returned to Linhay and she went back to Sheffield to begin the removal process. She'd successfully managed to purchase the Parfitt's house. Baxter informed me that not only had Mrs Baxter been very interested in the possibility of a teaching position, but that she had telephoned the school the very next day and arranged an interview. Two days later she had been to visit and fallen in love with it all. She'd been offered the job on the spot and once the building and cleanup were completed, she would start her new job. Baxter was over the moon, as was I.

I do so love a happy ending.

ABOUT THE AUTHOR

J. NEW IS THE AUTHOR of The Yellow Cottage Vintage Mysteries, traditional English whodunits with a twist, set in the 1930's. Known for their clever humour as well as the interesting slant on the traditional whodunit, they have all achieved Bestseller status on Amazon.

J. New also writes the Finch and Fischer contemporary cozy crime series and (coming in 2021) the Will Sharpe Mysteries set in her hometown during the 1960's. Her books have sold over one hundred-thousand copies worldwide.

Jacquie was born in West Yorkshire, England. She studied art and design and after qualifying began work as an interior designer, moving onto fine art restoration and animal portraiture before making the decision to pursue her lifelong ambition to write. She now writes full time and lives with her partner of twenty-one years, two dogs and five cats, all of whom she rescued.

IF YOU ENJOYED *A Double Life*, please consider leaving a review on Amazon.

IF YOU WOULD LIKE TO be kept up to date with new releases from J. New, you can sign up to her *Reader's Group* on her website www.jnewwrites.com[1] You will also receive a link to download the free e-book, *The Yellow Cottage Mystery*, the short-story prequel to the series.

Made in the USA
Monee, IL
22 August 2020